See You in Eden

THE SHORT STORIES OF LEONID PEKAROVSKY

See You in Eden – The Short Stories of Leonid Pekarovsky
Author: Leonid Pekarovsky
Translated from the Hebrew by Yaron Regev
Cover Design by Pen2Publishing and Svetlana Pekarovsky
Copyright © 2024 Leonid Pekarovsky

For all other information and permissions, please contact the author at: leonidpekarovsky@gmail.com

Table of Contents

Broom

Understand, I have a doctorate. I have invested many efforts in studying the Northern Renaissance. To be more precise—I was especially interested in the aesthetic aspect of Abrecht Durer's work—that mysterious genius who lived in the twilight of Germany's Middle Ages. Now here I am, cleaning streets in Tel Aviv. And there's more than enough trash to go around, thank God, which means I am able to regularly earn my daily bread.

Each morning, at the crack of dawn, when the dark, thick skies are painted by the colors of a modest sunrise which gradually deepen into a blue abyss, I set out to slowly tread the empty streets of Tel Aviv, pushing a cart with the instruments of my new trade: two trash cans, a broom and a dustpan. The sounds of the bird chorus, and the mysterious Cezanne-like shadows slowly oozing from the sidewalks into the yards, accelerate neural activity, creating in me an intense desire for deep thinking. Believe me, I mean just what I say. After all, my initial idea that thinking is as ceaseless and infinite a process as the universe itself, and just as independent of us, had proven to be ill-conceived.

There was a time—the first days and months in this, my new job—when I began to believe my thought-manufacturing mechanism had somehow been broken, and it was only on the inside, from afar, that it continued to watch me—an object in space, dressed in a Tel Aviv municipality uniform vigorously swinging a broom. The world shrank to the size of elementary objects, and had become as rigid as a mountain range. Gone were all deliberations, nuances, shades, and fine transformations of psychological flavors. And it was only in the dark and bitter nights, when my head ached maddeningly after suffering a sudden and uncalled for awakening, that I

1

dared to measure the exact magnitude of my fall into the abyss. The amount of pain per heart millimeter. The necessary temperature for willpower to evaporate from the surface of the soul, and the external pressure necessary to break it.

Once upon a time… time slowly slid over the murky surface of the Jordan River. Time, that professional burnisher, sheaved off from my world the sharp thorns that had wounded my heart to blood. Dust settled, and Goethe's obscure sentence, *"If you can't do what you love—love what you do,"* had become distinctly clear for me. Believe it or not—I actually began to love the broom! Not a single, particular broom, as if it was a work of art, but the idea of the broom. I discovered something that would once have seemed a terrible heresy: a broom can be a serious object of thought!

Actually, I wonder what is so heretical about this if we know that each object (in Plato's case, for instance, "the bench") can be described in an abstract way. Back when I was studying Durer's aesthetics, there was no way such a revelation would come easily to my mind. But when it did, it was this very revelation that restored me to a world glistening with colors and filled with scents. This new, rehabilitating consciousness realigned objects in a precise hierarchical line. The lowest level consisted of trash—various Coke and Pepsi cans, discarded papers, apple cores and banana peels, plastic bags, dried leaves and common dirt. Then, at eye level, newspaper stands, shop windows, the peeling walls of houses, people, cars and markets. Finally, the top level—if you raised your head to look up—a frozen dome of heaven, with a problematic reality higher still, and beyond… the precipice of the abyss, with God behind it, where human reason could gain no access and faith alone governs.

I was filled with a desire to sort out my new and special notions, so I conducted a little research into the history of the broom. And, as my list of sources was limited, results were fairly modest. But even these offered the opportunity to discover the footprints, though they were barely visible to the eye, the broom had left in its wake throughout the history of human evolution.

First, I tried to dig too deep, and found that my historical research could not penetrate past the Stone and Bronze Ages (from the twelfth to the fourth millennia BC). In all the primordial wall paintings depicting various animals (a deer, a bison, a lion, a mammoth) and weapons (bows, arrows, spears and stone axes), there wasn't a single broom to be found. I was also unable to find the image of a broom in the subtle art of Mesopotamia (moving up through time from the twenty-seventh to the twentieth century BC). The broom's existence in the countries of Sumer, Babylon and Assyria can only be guessed at, based on the palace paintings, depicting perfect cleanliness and numerous servants.

And then there they finally were, those obscure traces. I discovered them in the art of ancient Egypt. In the Middle Kingdom period, to be more precise (the nineteenth to the twenty-first centuries BC). Specifically, I found the first footprint in a painting on the grave of King Rahmira in Thebes. In a scene depicting a feast. Among the female dancers, a girl had been painted with a broom in her hand. The shape of the broom, echoing the soft contours of the shapely female servant, is drawn with an airy line that barely touches the surface of the wall. Could this subtle creation of classical art identify with a powerful workman's broom used to intimidate the dirty streets of a modern city? Yes indeed, ladies and gentlemen, the forefather of the tribe stands before you.

After that one revelatory find, the footprints vanish for many ages. I found them again in the art of Ancient Greece, in a late classical period (fifth century BC). On a vase, an image depicting *"Dionysus and his entourage"* had been painted, quite schematically, by some long-departed artist. In it a broom can be seen, symbolizing bodily cleanliness.

But it was Rome alone, where the rational thinking of ancient times reached its full fruition, that answered all the questions that intrigued me. In the excavations of Pompei, Herculaneum and Stabia, all consumed in 79 BC by the now frozen lava that had belched from Mount Vesuvius, archeologists found an abundance of well-preserved household objects. Among them, ovens, buckets, tables and benches ... and a broom. Roman genius and ingenuity had improved that ancient artifact beyond recognition so that in later periods—the early and late Middle Ages, the Renaissance, and modern history—nothing of significance has been added to the broom's architectural qualities. It has remained that same stick, tailored to suit the proportions of human beings, and ending with a rounded tip. The same brush comprised of thin, dry branches that narrowed as they descended toward the floor, and tied with a rope. But, aesthetically, the modern broom is not as pleasing to the eye as those of ancient Rome, where the stick would be adorned with delicate floral carvings...

These were the results of my little research. For me, who feels history so acutely, they bring a sense of mystery and importance. *Damn*, I sometimes think while stopping for a quick rest. *You, my dear, are a relative of the wheel and the pottery wheel.* And my heart fills to the brim with love. And the burdensome tiredness retreats beyond the murky wall of Tel Aviv's heat, and the trees, crumbling merciless sunbeams, scatter glittering gold dust on the sidewalk, and the honking, the screeching tires, the screaming, and the construction site noises, are all suddenly harmonious and blend into a wider music that grabs the broom. And it breaks into a passionate dance, leaping in elaborate movements, leaving behind it a pure white trail...

I am the broom dance choreographer. Its current airy, animated dance is a result of my many efforts to master the technique of sweeping. You smile? You think this business requires nothing but a simple pendulum motion—back and forth? Believe me, you are wrong. Take the word of a professional.

The choice of the broom itself is crucial. Call me unpatriotic, but I prefer the Italian professionals. Knowledge comes with experience, and I've had my fair share of troubles with the "Israeli's." They're heavy and clumsy, with bodies devoid of elasticity and springiness. Without question, in certain conditions they are unmatched, like when you need a large broom mass for sweeping leaves off a wet sidewalk, or to create an added wind effect to accelerate the flight of trash. Yet ... still ... the excess weight of Israeli brooms, and the stiffness of their construction, limits the freedom of movement and brings on tiredness quickly.

They cannot possibly be compared with "Italians," which are shapely and refined. Their airiness and incredible flexibility allow you to perform minor miracles. Their responsiveness and spontaneity allow you to easily change your sweeping style. For example, "the springy sweep," which allows maximum saving of the sweeper's strength. In this case, the broom's body first bends at its hips, then sharply straightens and hurls the trash a meter or two away.

"The measured sweep" is brief, energetic and precise. It is necessary when the cleaning process nears the finish line, a pile has been formed, and maximum precision is required to reach a certain point.

The exact opposite of the measured sweep is the "return sweep," used when you need to remove trash from places that are difficult to reach. In these cases, you need to work with the broom in movements that lead not away from you, but toward you, with a short and precise swing amplitude.

It is, though, the "diagonal sweep" that gives me the greatest pleasure. I have mastered it to perfection. This is when I aim the broom like a professional hockey player manipulating a ball with his stick. The sweep is executed by swinging right and left (you grab it either from the right or left side) at an angle of slightly less than ninety degrees from the surface of the sidewalk. This is an aesthetically beautiful method, as the quick way of working, combined with the constant change in the way the stick is grabbed—right hand up and left hand down, then the other way around—creates the illusion of a virtuosic juggling act.

Well, this little research, what is it all about? Is it about the broom? Most definitely not. It is about my soul looking for justification. But a broom too, if I may say—when on Israel's soil, is far more than a broom.

Umbrella

I admit it—I'm a junkie! If I don't get my fix in the morning, I feel sick all day, and tormented by bitter feelings. The drug I've been addicted to for many years is not morphine, nor is it heroin. It's books. And I shoot them straight into my brain. There, the drug is absorbed by my intellect and penetrates my heart and my soul. In the next stage, my drugged consciousness, ready for the metaphysical journey, holds its breath. It takes me far-far over the Earth, way up high above the clouds—assuming, of course, that there are actually clouds at that particular moment in the utterly faded Tel Aviv summer sky.

Well, it is eight times now that I've read all the books in my little library, the ones I brought with me from the diaspora to the Land of Israel. As for new books, I cannot afford to buy them, as they are very expensive and I am a poor man! No, my poverty isn't absolute, of the kind when you have nothing to eat, your clothes are tattered and torn, and you sit in the old central bus station begging for alms. I am relatively poor, because as a guard I earn a minimum wage and can barely make ends meet. After paying all the bills—mortgage, property taxes, electricity, water, telephone and gas—there's still a little left for some food and inexpensive clothes I buy from a clearance boutique. Forget about classical music concerts which purify the soul, or buying a book I have long been dreaming about, like, for example, *Creative Evolution* by Henri Bergson.

One day, I found that book at a chain bookstore in Allenby Street. I was filled with lust for it as I skimmed over the introduction. I read, *"The book* Creative Evolution, *published in 1907, has earned Bergson world renown as a thinking man and an author. It is mainly due to this publication that he won the Nobel Prize for literature in 1927..."*

In my youth, I had wanted to be a thinker, a philosopher, but no philosopher had emerged from me, because of my limited mental capacity. I admired the great Schopenhauer, and Nietzsche. Both had been genius philosophers and accomplished writers. Now I stood in that bookstore in Allenby with Henri Bergson's book in my hands. I turned to the back cover and looked at the price. The blow to my financial consciousness was immediate and crushing. There was no way I could have bought it...

And now here I am, sitting in my guard booth, thinking about Henri Bergson and his book *Creative Evolution*. I am wondering how I can get my hands on this book. How? How could I do it without draining our meager family budget? At the same time, with an unfocused gaze, my eyes skim over the objects that are with me in the guard booth. Over the years, I have become so used to them that I feel they are close to my heart. A radio tape—I listen to the Russian channel on it. An electric kettle—I make a brew five times a day; three cups of tea and two cups of black coffee. Three windows. Above them, there are shutters I open or close, according to where the sun is in the sky as it moves on its circular course above Tel Aviv. To my right, on a hook, hangs an umbrella.

Stop!

I jerk myself back to reality and focus my total attention on that umbrella. It is black, a child's umbrella, a small one. Someone had forgotten to take it with them about eight years ago. I had hung it in my guard booth thinking that should anyone remember the loss, and come to claim it, I would be able to return the umbrella. But no one ever has. Which is how it has gained its place here for all time, among the other items in the booth. That umbrella, if a child is not playing with it, is of no use at all. Once, I tried to use it in heavy rain. My head remained dry, but my back was completely soaked. So I just put the umbrella aside. It was the only object in the booth that didn't have a job.

Perhaps the other objects considered it to be a parasite. I don't know. But over time, I had gradually gotten used to that umbrella, and now I can no longer imagine an inner view of the booth without it. Umbrella... Umbrella... Then I had a sudden revelation, and in that instant an idea was born that seemed utterly brilliant. An umbrella can be used for protection, not only from the rain, but also from the sun. Furthermore, it was invented some 3,000 years ago in China or Egypt (historians cannot seem to come to an agreement regarding which) as a means of protection from the sun. What if I added an additional service to my job, accompanying the company's employees and customers holding the black umbrella from my booth over their heads? First, this would protect them from the scorching Israeli sun, blazing and sparklingly blinding. And second, it would add an aristocratic finesse to the way the company's clients were welcomed, which might, in turn, influence their mood, and to a certain degree even their decision of whether or not to purchase an expensive product, i.e., a vehicle.

The idea seemed revolutionary to me, because no parking lot in Israel offered a service like it. And, of course, it would be provided free of charge. But I have to admit, deep in my soul, in its darkest recesses, a dim hope stirred. Perhaps someone would feel they should tip me for this "gratis" service. Small change, perhaps, but over time, if I let it accumulate long enough, it would allow me to save the money for me to purchase Henri Bergson's *Creative Evolution*...

The next day, at about nine in the morning, my first customer arrives. He gets out of his car. He looks to be in his mid-forties, curly hair. His skin tanned enough to be deemed unafraid of the blazing Israeli sun. A man who does not normally use sun lotion, or visit a dermatologist to have the dangers of skin cancer clearly explained.

I open the umbrella and take a step towards him. He smiles sarcastically and says, "But it's summer, not winter. What do you need an umbrella for?"

I explain to him, in all seriousness, that in a company like ours the umbrella is an additional service, aimed at protecting the client from the insufferable summer sun on his way from the car to the building.

I open the umbrella over his head. He removes my umbrella-holding hand, obviously seeing this whole situation as a miserable joke, or, even worse—as mockery and derision.

"What, can't you tell by my tan that I'm not afraid of a little sun?"

"The skin is one thing," I say, "but the sun's rays also strike at the head like a hammer."

"I have a strong head. It could even take a blow from a real hammer."

I stand there looking at the customer. I have to overcome his skepticism and distrust. I am convinced my revolutionary idea will work. I call on my imagination to help. It obediently comes, bringing inspiration with it. In bright, verbal, colors, I begin to recount the history of the umbrella. I tell the client, who first listens to me incredulously, then with growing interest, that the nation that gave birth to the umbrella was either China or Egypt—no one has yet been able to determine with certainty which exactly. Along with the fan, to have one was considered a privilege reserved solely for monarchs and ministers. It was invented somewhere around the eleventh century BC, and was used exclusively for protection against the sun.

From the east, use of the umbrella spread west until it reached ancient Greece. From there it migrated to Rome—where it was mainly used by women. It was only in the eighteenth century that the umbrella was used for protection against rain.

"For our clients who don't need protection from the sun," I add on a final note, "we offer this service to stress just how much we respect them, and how much we appreciate the fact that they come to us."

I stop speaking. The customer, overwhelmed by that torrent of tumultuous information, is left shocked. But upon hearing my last words, about the great honor bestowed upon him by the company, and about all the appreciation we have for him, he snaps out of his state of shock.

"I'm ready!" he says. "And just how much does this service cost?"

"It costs nothing."

By this time, he is utterly appeased. We start marching, with me holding the umbrella over his head. You should have seen how he walks the twenty meters from the parking lot to the building. He holds his chest out, lifts his head, and his gait has suddenly become regal and calculated, like that of a Chinese Mandarin. His self-appreciation has swelled to humungous proportions. When we reach the entrance to the building, he pats my shoulder and says:

"Thank you, old boy! Your company certainly has excellent customer service."

In that same way, I serve three more customers like him. Towards noon, the fifth one arrives. Not very young. Fairly tall. With a beautiful white beard, echoing Ernest Hemingway's. His skin testifies to the fact that he hasn't been made for exposure to sunlight. I notice little red lumps on his hands, and pigment stains. I tell him about our new service. His face fills with a boundless expression of self-importance, as if he is telling me, "If such a service exists in your company, then serve me!"

Before he goes into the building, he throws me a quick, "Thank you," and extends a coin to me. One shekel. And that is how I discover the cost of this service I have invented: one shekel.

Over the course of three hot summer months that transform Tel Aviv into a kind of inferno, I run with the childish umbrella back and forth across the concrete lot. My idea has proven to be a little less brilliant than I originally thought. True, I have received tips, but only in the following proportion—out of every ten customers, only two have given me a shekel. But even that has been enough for me to save, over the summer, the necessary amount.

At the end of September, when Rosh Hashana is drawing near, I arrange a holiday gift for myself. I buy the book, *Creative Evolution* by Henri Bergson. In the first two days that follow, I sniff exaggerated doses of the drug. In other words, I read fervently. Under the influence of that foggy intoxication, I have completely forgotten about running back and forth across the scorching parking lot and the humiliation of marching with an umbrella in one hand, holding it over the heads of the customers bobbing beneath it.

And how could I not forget all that with such a powerful dosage penetrating straight into my sensitive brain. For example: *"... the more he advances down the trajectory of time, the mental state grows wider, due to the dimension it absorbs: as if he rolls within himself like a snowball..."*

Next summer, I intend to repeat my tiny business within a business so I will be able to buy myself another book for Rosh Hashana. This time it will be *Conversations with Goethe*, by Johann Peter Eckermann.

Shoes

Dedicated to my son

I believe that everything is preordained. That free will does not exist. That each second of my life has been prewritten in the fascinating book of my fate, and that it was written before I came into the world. I believe that I have no true way of choosing, and I tread the path that has been decided for me. As Baruch Spinoza described it in his divine wisdom:

"Each man wishes and acts as God, since the dawn of time, has ordained that he should desire and act. Yet how this accords with man's freedom—that is beyond our reason..."

Indeed, it is beyond my reason as well. If I could reconcile all of God's decisions, regarding my fate, with man's free will, I would have had no problem explaining all that happened to me yesterday and today.

This is how it happened.

Yesterday, I was sitting in my guard booth on La Guardia Street in Tel Aviv. The booth is located right over the bustling road, and the powerful winds blowing in from the Mediterranean rattle it constantly. Those same winds hurled a large cardboard box into the road. I saw it was a television box—and it was creating a dangerous situation. Cars swerved past the box at great speed, cutting across into each other's lanes. I sat and watched, and I thought to myself that perhaps the box should be removed—but that would be dangerous. Extremely dangerous! Still, some unexplained power gripped me and moved me from my booth. And it didn't stop at that, it kept right on pushing, forcing me towards the road even as, all the time, my subconscious was whispering inside my head, *Don't go! Don't go! You'll end up dead!*

There was an instant when traffic eased a bit, and the way to the box appeared momentarily safer, or at least it seemed to be so in my eyes. I started across the road. Suddenly, from beyond the turn— from the highway to La Guardia Street—a bus emerged. I, wearing a guard's uniform, an official entity performing his duty, assumed that holding up my hand with all five fingers spread would be enough to make the bus driver stop to allow me to quickly dash across the road and reach the box.

It didn't happen that way! He kept on driving as if I wasn't even there. What's more, he put his foot down on the gas pedal to try to cross the intersection before the yellow light blinked to red. I barely managed to escape from under the front left wheel. I scrambled over to the box, snatched it up, and ran quickly back to shove it into the trash container.

A single second was enough for me to register the face of my failed assassin for all time. A pudgy nose underlined by a mustache. Black, curly locks coiled across the forehead.

Now, as I write these lines, I imagine I had even seen little horns poking from between those locks…

Back in the booth, my heart was pounding so hard I felt it would rip through my chest and fall to roll on the floor. I had had quite a scare. *Do you know where you have just been?* I asked myself. *At the gates of death!* I answered silently.

But it was all forgotten before evening fell. I think it is my greatest skill, forgetting. When Antisthenes, the Greek philosopher, was asked which is the most necessary of sciences, he replied, "The science of forgetfulness." I, too have forgotten.

I had an important meeting scheduled for the next day, and my mind had been constantly occupied with it. Three days earlier, as I had been sitting serenely on the sofa with my wife, watching a Russian television channel, the phone rang. A soft, feminine voice asked, "Are you Leonid?" and, following my confirmation, introduced its owner. She was, apparently, an editor with one of Israel's finest, longstanding publishers. She told me she had read some of my stories in the newspaper, and so had her boss. The latter, after coming across my last story, had been so enthralled with what he'd read that he immediately asked her to locate me and schedule an appointment. They wanted, so she told me, to publish a collection of my short stories. She had found my telephone number through information, and now here she was, talking to me on the telephone. We had scheduled an appointment, which was supposed to take place this very day, from 3:00 p.m. to 5:00 p.m.

My wife asked me who had been on the line. I told her it was an editor for a large publisher, that they wanted to publish a book of my stories, and that we had scheduled an appointment. She sank into deep thought, then said, "You need to dress nicely. You know very well you get no second chance to make a first impression!"

She went into the bedroom, opened the closet and brought back cappuccino-colored velvet pants, a loose American shirt, and my holiday shoes.

On the rare occasions when I think of those shoes, I somehow always seem to enter a poetic mood, with a touch of daydreaming. Each time I remember how I had gotten them, I am overwhelmed by a wave of gentle, fatherly emotions, and even an occasional tear will moisten my eyes.

The shoes had been a birthday present from my son. He had brought them from America where he had been on a business trip. In the very last minutes of his stay in New York, on the verge of missing his flight, he found the time to quickly go to one of the expensive stores and buy me a pair of shoes for my birthday. This gesture had warmed my heart in a very special way.

Now—a few words about the shoes themselves. They had been manufactured by Kimberland, and manufactured like none other! The pattern was particularly refined, the artistic shape perfect—and how subtle the contours that blended together so harmoniously. And then there were the colors! A bright and airy suede that seemed to melt into the thicker, darker brown shade of the sole. Together, they formed a spectacularly soft spectrum of colors. The sole had been designed using the latest technology, the chemical composition making them both sturdy and viscid. When I wore them, I always had the fanciful notion that I was not walking, but hovering a few centimeters above the ground, a little air cushion between the asphalt and the sole...

Those shoes were so precious to me that I rarely wore them. They came out only for weddings, births, bar-mitzvahs, birthdays, Passovers and for the first of May, the International Workers' Day. And that because I viewed myself, a guard watching over capitalist property, as part of the world proletariat.

And so, on the eve of my appointment with one of Israel's most prestigious book publishers, my wife got out the velvet pants, a loose American shirt, and my beloved Kimberland suede shoes.

That morning heavy rain had been falling, so I decided not to wear my holiday shoes and wore regular sneakers instead. Mundane shoes. I put the expensive ones in a bag, thinking I would change into them just before going into the meeting. There were two other bags, one filled with trash, the other held a broken coffee machine. I took my briefcase and the three bags and left the house. I locked the door. I went down to the ground floor in the elevator. It is only now, looking back, I realize I had not been aware of my own actions. I was detached from reality because my mind was fully occupied by the coming meeting. How would I speak to these high-minded intellectuals? In my broken Hebrew, which was barely enough for me to breathe, or, to be more accurate, gasp for breath?

I had gone into the garbage room, where two trash containers stood, and dumped the bags in one of the two. Then I had gone on to work.

An hour passed. I was sitting in my booth, listening to the radio, to a news bulletin. Suddenly, from out of nowhere, the thought struck me. *Where is the bag with my shoes? Where are the shoes?* I was instantly sheened in cold sweat. I grabbed the telephone.

"Sveta!" I shouted into the mouthpiece at my wife.

"What? What's happened?" she answered, panic in her voice.

"I threw the shoes in the garbage!" I blurted. "Hurry! Go! Run!" And she ran. For the next five minutes I sat... and sat... and... The phone rang. I snatched at the receiver.

"I ran all the way down, but they had just emptied the containers into the garbage truck..."

I sat, unmoving, for half an hour. Turned to stone. Then an idea flashed into my mind. A spark that ignited my imagination. I realized that what had happened this morning with the shoes ... now there was a wonderful plot for a little story. And writing it immediately would, I thought, diminish the pain of the loss. After all, it is a well-known fact that art is the best medicine for an aching soul.

I began to write, connecting everything that had happened into a single structure; my thoughts about the lack of free will and that each step we take is preordained, the incident with the box on the road, how I had been miraculously saved from being crushed by the wheels of the bus, and then—payment for my stupidity, the stupidity that had nearly cost me my life. Payment rendered in the form of the mistake I had made when I tossed the shoes into the trash container. I thought it lucky the payment hadn't demanded a price that might have affected my good health, or my wallet with all my money and credit cards...

Now, I should say here that two charming people met me at the publisher's office, Ora and Avi, the elite of Israeli intellectuals. They spoke such perfect Hebrew that my mouth turned sweet, as if I had just eaten a fine, Belgian chocolate bar. They could not have cared less about how I was dressed. They did not even glance at my sneakers, and I still don't understand why I kept them hidden under the table.

Well, that's it, my story's done. But before I end, it is important that I express my hopes. Perhaps I'll manage to sell this story to one of Israel's most prestigious newspapers. I do not rule out the possibility that they would pay me generously for it. If they do, I'll take the payment, and go to Tel Aviv to buy myself a pair of Kimberland shoes. Just like the ones I tossed into the trash container.

Portrait

"The portrait appeared to be unfinished, but the power of the handling was striking."

                                    - N. Gogol, *The Mysterious Portrait*

Sometimes, he would take the portrait from the folder in which he kept his youthful poetry, and gaze at it for a long time. Doting over it, reminiscing. It was a portrait of his sexual organ. Life-size. The drawing was in the classical style, with each detail drawn to such a refined level of final lines, that the whole shone with the entrancing glow of perfect harmony. And the play of light and shadow had been done with such skill, that the black seemed to undergo an entire spectrum of shade shifting, all imaginary, of course, from an airy, pearly pink, to the slightly more intense pink of a ripening raspberry, then deeper still, until it took on the shade of a red, ripened cherry. Finally, it was the color of congealed blood—the color the head of any male member becomes on the verge of the final moments of ecstasy and ejaculation.

The style of the portrait leaned towards the German school of painting, of the Northern Renaissance—European, in the Albrecht Dürer vein. In other words, it touched upon the clean-cut shape, and the lines that form it, which so distinctly obeyed the artist's will-power and firm hand, reflecting his every whim. And, after all, he was familiar with that hand. It was that hand, not the eyes, that were the mirror of the soul. It was possible to speak of the cool asceticism of the dry palm, and the long, chiseled fingers. But with what amazing speed did they rush to fill, to the tips and the fingernails, with a passionate blaze and a warm quiver, as they took hold of his member, larger now, but yet to achieve its final rigidity.

That transitional state exercised a magical influence over the owner of the hand, and she was able to pluck, for an indefinite amount of time, like the strings of a harp, the sprawling member—the testicles as well. She bewitched. She cast spells. She pressed it to her cheek, or suddenly, with the sharp blade of her tongue, touched those little, oh-so-sensitive, fleshy parts. He shuddered... Sometimes, at the moment of climax, just when his member was filled with blood, the fire of his lover's religious admiration suddenly dimmed, was even extinguished, in her eyes, and she measured him with an artist's cold gaze.

In those moments he would cease to be a symbol and become an object of observation. But even then, even as she was thinking, comparing, analyzing for the umpteenth time, she was amazed at just how much his member transcended, in its artistic qualities, all the other objects she was familiar with—a tree, or even a face. That perfect construct (in the moments when it was erect, of course). That golden ratio of the dome, as defined in Ancient Greece; the virtuosic connection between the dome and the stem, all covered by the velvet of the foreskin (assuming the member is uncircumcised) as well as the countless variations of ornamental color formed by the interweaving of capillaries.

Unusual metamorphoses took place with the light. First, its intensity was swallowed into the member, and then, after being wrapped in it by the energy of life sent by God himself, it shone outside.

That is the reason, she thought, *that a light emanates from the head, reminiscent of a halo.*

A desire to draw it had suddenly taken hold of her. In the first session, she sat, Indian style, in front of the erect member, which he held in his hand. She placed on her easel a piece of thick cardboard with coarse paper attached, and started sketching a portrait of the member with a black, Italian pencil. She worked with a kind of fervent passion, and treated the member as she would a living model whose image had to be copied onto the page. Meanwhile, the erectness of the member had inevitably relaxed somewhat, waned, and he frequently had to bolster its tumescence by putting out a foot, easing it under the cardboard to search between her legs with his toe, to feel her thick pubic hair, her vagina—which moistened—and then, with a little luck, her clitoris too, which he had to spend some time searching for.

Inflamed, washed through with waves of desire, she would hurl aside the cardboard holding the drawing, and lunge at him. They would roll on the bed over and over, then slide down to the floor...

There were many sessions. The first renderings were unsatisfactory to her. The direct interpretation of the model created a sort of general form which was almost lifeless. The virtuosic drawing, despite being well executed, came out somewhat dry, she thought, evoking echoes of the dried-up academic school. Perhaps she had erred with something. Yes—yes! Her mistake was inherent in the idea itself. She, for some reason, had decided that the essence of the male member, its plethora of mysterious varieties, its elusive contours that were ceaselessly changing, could be communicated only by the use of an artistic technique, the focus being only on the forms, the lines and the way the light played on the surface of mass and volume.

But, when all was said and done, the member ought to be seen as a unique organ of desire. After all, it was that burning hot, pointed column of turgid flesh that penetrated her body. Marvelously intense, uninhibited, perhaps a little rough sometimes, causing a sweet pain that quickly passed. Yet at the same time, it could be gentle, caressing, willing to make self-sacrifices, and bearing, in itself, her happiness and greatest satisfaction. *What,* she wondered, *has been the object of my dreams since youthhood, when I secretly read daring books and my hand felt for those familiar places beneath the childhood panties?*

When she thought like that about the male member, her imagination was pleasantly stimulated. And not just in a creative way. She was also overwhelmed by a powerfully erotic stimulus that was even more inflamed by her imagination. The portrait would be filled with life, and only then did the complex game of colors begin to manifest itself beneath the black pencil strokes, and the lines began to fill with real blood, throbbing like a vein pulsing in a temple.

The principle of composition she borrowed from the great painters of the past: Leonardo, Ingres and Delacroix. That principle was based on a sense of how the portrait should be finished, with the more important details of the drawing honed to maximum perfection, and then the contours of the supporting parts of the composition would weaken, the lines becoming a mere hint, melting in the encoded secret. Slowly, gradually, getting lost in the white mists of the paper's silence.

The member, drawn without testicles, which made it appear rootless, hovered at the top of the page. If the eye slid over it from the bottom up, it gave the illusion of taking flight into eternity. And if one looked at it from top to bottom, it appeared to plunge into a prehistoric era that preceded life itself...

Occasionally, he would take the portrait out and look at it at length, with the eyes of a fastidious art expert. Like a constricted throat, the memories would then roll over him. Suddenly, from the black pit of the past, from the reddish glow of autumn, her vague figure would emerge. Then the image would evaporate—its place taken by a sensation familiar only to rich collectors who have gained possession of a stolen masterpiece painted by a genius artist. It was the sensation of taking pleasure in the secret ownership of an illicit masterpiece. Once sated, he would hide the portrait again, back in its folder.

The Donut

The rat passed away suddenly, on the holiday of Hanukkah.

As I wrote the first sentence of the story, I immediately noticed two inaccuracies. First, it is wrong to say that an animal "passed away"; we reserve that phrase for human beings. Instead, when referring to a beloved animal—be it our dog or our cat—we say that it "died." This also holds true for the kindhearted and wonderfully clever old rat who was beloved by every rat living in Tel Aviv.

Secondly, when I wrote that the rat had passed away suddenly, I demonstrated a complete lack of understanding regarding the essence of death. Death cannot be sudden or random; it always arrives just in time—at the day and hour appointed in advance. The words "the rat passed away suddenly" contain the very essence of inaccuracy, and I plead guilty as charged.

Now, what do we know about this rat? Not much. She had been born and raised in one of the kibbutzim, where the air was rife with socialist, communal ideas. So much so that during the years of the Second World War, a portrait of Stalin proudly hung in the communal dining hall. Then the rat left the kibbutz and found herself in Tel Aviv, where, at the time, the city that never sleeps was home to seventy-five thousand rats.

Our rat quickly ascended the ranks of the rat community's leadership.

However, beyond these facts, the rest of her life remains enshrouded in mystery, as rats live in a parallel world unknown to humans.

That Hanukkah evening, for reasons known only to her, the rat had arrived in downtown Tel Aviv, at 10 Dubnov Street, perhaps seeking to enter Café Alternative, where she had already visited

21

many times. She made her way into the café through the kitchen and found a plate full of enticing Hanukkah donuts on the bar counter. In a few seconds, the rat would start gnawing on the donuts, even though she knew she shouldn't. The elderly rat suffered from severe diabetes, and her heart and liver were not in good shape either.

Now, let's take a moment to explore what a Hanukkah donut, or *"sufganiyah"* in Hebrew, is exactly, and how it affects your heart.

The earliest mention of a dough-baked donut appears in the writings of Rabbi Maimon ben Joseph, Maimonides' father, who lived in the twelfth century: "The custom of *al-sfenj* should not be taken lightly, and it is an ancient custom." The *sfenj* that Rabbi Maimon ben Joseph referred to is a kind of sweet fritter, a prototype of the modern donut. As for the round Hanukkah donut, stuffed with jam, it is an invention of Western civilization dating back to the year 1485. In the pages of the first cookbook in history, printed on Johannes Gutenberg's printing press, there is a recipe for *"Gefüllte Krapfen"*: a fritter made of two dough circles, fried in pork fat, and stuffed with ham in the middle. The Jews replaced the pork fat with goose fat, and the *"Gefüllte Krapfen"* turned into the Hanukkah donut. The process of making the donut also influenced the invention of its Hebrew name—*Sufganiyah*. Like many words in the modern Hebrew language, it is comparatively new but has roots planted deep in the past. The word *"sfog"*—sponge exists in both ancient and modern Hebrew, and the Hanukkah donut soaks in oil like a sponge.

This abundance of fat in the donut causes many people, especially those who prefer healthy nutrition, to refuse to touch this particular food during Hanukkah. However, this was not always the case in days of old. This is why Rabbi Maimon ben Joseph does not explicitly insist but merely tries to convince those who are not among the followers of the donut, saying that the custom of eating them on Hanukkah is not to be taken lightly.

In other words, the custom of not eating donuts during Hanukkah is just as old as the custom of eating them. This allowed Rabbi

Litzman, a man of great ideas who served as vice minister of health in Israel at the time of the rat's death, to publicly declare that it is unhealthy to eat donuts and that consuming them can harm people's health... and that of rats, as we will soon see for ourselves. The old rat was well aware of Rabbi Litzman's call not to eat donuts. In that case, why had she eaten one? Well, how can one resist the wonder of culinary arts? Like Venus rising from the sea, the Hanukkah donut rises from the boiling oil: so airy, fragrant, and perfectly round. It melts in one's mouth with joyful glee, filling it with the special taste of the airy dough soaked with oil and the flavor of the jam. It evokes a feeling of pleasure that cannot be compared to anything else, becoming a culinary ecstasy that can no longer be controlled.

The rat could not resist the temptation. She bit into the donut over and over with little nibbles, using the only yellow fang she still had remaining and her two incisors. The bits of donut gently melted in the rat's gullet. She chewed at breakneck speed and even closed her eyes with pleasure, daydreaming as she recalled her childhood in the kibbutz, where they spoiled themselves with donuts every Hanukkah, under the gaze of the mustached Stalin.

But then, after the rat had eaten half a donut, her stomach began to ache. The pain turned more acute by the second. She could no longer bear it. But it only appeared to her that her stomach was what was bothering her. No, in actuality it was the surplus of fat and sugar that had overwhelmed the rat's liver all at once. Her blood sugar level leapt to three hundred. She began to feel sharp pangs in her heart and a burning pain.

The rat started choking. Then she ceased to feel her hind legs and realized that this was it, this was the end. But no, not here. Not by the counter! She overcame the pain and started crawling towards the wall separating the space of the café and the lobby where I worked as a security guard. She squeezed through the crack between the wall and the floor and, in one of the empty concrete cavities, met her demise.

A day or two later, the stifling smell of a carcass spread in the lobby. A maintenance employee named Moshe was sent to investigate. He broke the part of the wall made of plaster, yet found nothing. He reached the part made of concrete and ultimately gave up. Then they redid the part of the wall made of plaster. The smell of the rotting rat continued to fill the lobby, but two weeks later, it suddenly vanished.

What had happened? Had the body decomposed in such a short time? No! The dead rat was retrieved from her concrete tomb. A special group of rat researchers had labored for two weeks in order to track the rat's final Tel Aviv journey and locate her final resting place: the concrete part of the wall separating Café Alternative and the lobby of the building where I worked as a guard. At night, no less than five of them arrived, rescued the rat from the wall, and dragged her via underground routes all the way to the Tel Aviv rat cemetery. There, in the rat's funeral, five thousand rats convened. Representatives from various kibbutzim had arrived, as well as delegates from various cities in central Israel: Rishon LeZion, Holon, Bat Yam. Emotional eulogies were spoken, all full of pathos. Another female rat, about the same age as the deceased, born and grown in the same kibbutz, told the mourners with tears in her eyes how the departed possessed a strong character, even in her childhood. She had an insatiable thirst for knowledge and strived to help all those who needed aiding. The rat's fellow party members spoke of the departed rat's heroic struggles for the rights of the rat working class. And everyone recalled the famous words that same rat had used to say: "I must do as much good as I can for as many rats as possible!"

Then they interred the rat's body in the earth, and all the other rats scattered to their different ways in pensive slowness.

Albrecht Dürer

For Hadara

Professor Alexander Pashaver was a night watchman at the Electra factory in Rishon Lezion's new industrial area. In a previous life, which had evaporated never to return, like a soul from a corpse, he had managed one of the departments in the Hermitage Museum, and had lectured at the St. Petersburg Academy of the Arts. His knowledge of Northern Renaissance art was astounding in its depth and richness. However, when he had arrived in Israel, necessity had forced the professor to take a job as a simple night watchman.

When he was on duty at night, he sat in his guard's booth and busied himself writing a dissertation about Albrecht Dürer. He knew his efforts would come to nothing—no matter how well researched and written his dissertation might be, no one was going to publish it. Still, the professor persevered, justifying his endeavors with two motivating reasons. First, the act of thinking and writing sated, if only a little, his spirit, which had been drained by the stress of the merciless immigration process. Second, writing helped him to stay awake. He could not afford to be caught sleeping by the supervisor, for that could cost him his job.

Questions about Albrecht Dürer's art had occupied Pashaver's mind for a long time. Academic arguments regarding it had been raging on for nearly 300 years. Questions like which period did the genius artist belong to, late Gothic, or Northern European Renaissance? The professor was less than content with any of the existing theories. Not because they weren't true—absolutely not—but because of the sense he had that they were incomplete. He was also disturbed by the fact that the opposing theories did not appear, to him, to be contradictory. He wondered how that could be.

Pashaver distinctly remembered the evening when the basic idea had emerged in his mind in its entirety. It was the evening that Inspector Moshe Rubinstein, a retired IDF colonel and a former intelligence officer—tall, bald, with an ascetic face, metallic smile and a prickly demeanor—had told the professor that a watchman did not need to think, only carry out instructions. (Actually, he had said it even more pointedly. He had said a night watchman needed to be small-minded; in other words—brainless).

"You must make your rounds every hour, on the hour, and never, under any circumstances fall asleep!"

"Yes, yes, I understand," Pashaver muttered in an apologetic tone, though he had nothing to apologize for.

As soon as the retired colonel's black limousine had vanished around a corner of the building, the professor went into the guard booth, took a thick, ninety-six page notebook from his bag, opened it—and sank into deep thought. Without realizing what he was doing, he turned his face up towards the stars and the thin sliver of silver light that was the moon lying on its back. His eyes were open but he saw neither the moon nor the stars. His gaze was turned entirely inwards. And there the opposite was true. In his mind he saw! In his mind he felt he was heating up, illuminating what was happening, feeling, with the fingers of his mind, the tender, newly born idea...

In the seventeenth century, Pashaver thought, *Joachim von Sandrart wrote in his essay, "Teutsche Academie," that Dürer's creations were born of the Hellenistic Renaissance art. In the nineteenth century, the renowned Winckelmann, and the Swiss, Vulfin , further developed that theory.*

Opposing them had been the representatives of German romanticism—Herder and Wackenroder, and the Schlegel brothers. They had claimed that southern European influence had lowered the potential of German art, and classified Dürer as being part of the late Gothic period and the ancient German traditions...

The first night, Pashaver wrote nothing but the title. *"Certain Issues in A. Dürer's Aesthetics."* Over the course of the following nights, he walked along the perimeter fence and perfected, in his mind, the structure of his theory. Among his colleagues, the other security guards, the word was that Pashaver was a little soft in the head because he did not sleep on duty, not even on Fridays and Saturdays when the supervisor never ever showed his face.

Towards the end of the month, Pashaver felt he was ready and began putting his thoughts in writing. The more he progressed into the heart of the idea, the more interesting became the possibilities that opened up to him. For example, Heidrich, one of Vulfin's pupils, when he had been researching the Italian influences on Dürer, had remarked that the great painter had *"... processed southern European urges based on gothic traditions."* In so doing, Heidrich raised a theory regarding the dual existence (retrospective and progressive) of Dürer's art.

Pashaver expanded on this to add another layer to the duet of Gothic-Renaissance—the Reformation. At the heart of his idea was the *"correspondence principle."* He mentioned Shelling, who, in his essay, *"Von der Weltseele,"* (1797) had written that *"... the polarity between two opposing opinions can also be imaginary, and groups of opposing concepts are not actually opposed but merely complementing each other in describing the same phenomenon."* To support this determination, Pashaver drew on Niels Bohr—founder of the classic correspondence formula, *"The integrity of living organisms, the characteristics of sentient man and human cultures—these all require a complementary mode of description."*

Pashaver analyzed two basic, opposing movements in the history of aesthetic philosophy. The Platonic and the Aristotelian, both of which formed the theoretical basis for Gothic and Renaissance art, and lived in harmony in Dürer's art.

Writing about the Reformation period, the professor mentioned Erasmus of Rotterdam and his *"Diatribe,"* as well as Martin Luther's *"On the Bondage of the Will,"* which served as a reply to

Erasmus. He quoted Luther's letter to the lawman, Sheirel, in which the great reformer thanked Dürer for the paintings he had sent him. *"I received the gift of a great man, Albrecht Dürer. I would like you to relay my gratitude to the renowned Albrecht Dürer for this souvenir..."*

Pashaver constructed the arguments of his theory with such virtuosic skill that the theory itself was soon imbued with features of astonishing aesthetic beauty.

Finally, four months later, the night came when Pashaver's research was drawing to a close. He was wholly immersed in his writing—so it was of little surprise that he failed to notice, at 3:30 a.m., the supervisor arrive. That night it was Ofer. Twenty-two, tall and strong, Ofer had only recently been discharged from military service in the Parachute Brigade.

After he had waited a few minutes in the car, Ofer realized Pashaver was not going to emerge from the guard booth and he began to honk his horn. Jerking out of his concentrated study, Pashaver snatched up the security ledger he needed Ofer to sign, and lunged outside.

"Were you sleeping?" Ofer demanded bluntly.

"No, I wasn't asleep. I was just lost in thought and didn't hear your car arrive."

Ofer wrote in the security ledger that night watchman Alex Pashaver had been sleeping at the time of his inspection. Then he handed the ledger back to Pashaver, turned around and drove off.

The professor took it very hard, and perhaps that was why the final paragraph turned out to be less than impressive.

"Albrecht Dürer's artistic heritage is a boundless source of knowledge, and it is impossible to find answers to all the questions posed by this complex phenomenon. And that is why, in this current research, only a handful of the questions relating to the genius artist's aesthetics have been analyzed. His work awaits more and more generations of new researchers."

He firmly inscribed the very last period—and then fell fast asleep.

Ofer's remark in the ledger caused repercussions. At first, the bosses wanted to sack Pashaver, but then, for some reason, they seemed to take pity on him and allowed him to go on working in the guard's booth.

But they fined him a hundred and fifty shekels.

Schnitzels

Rachel Fidelman was about to go to Jerusalem, to visit her sister Sofa, who had undergone heart surgery. *I need to cheer up dear Sofa*, Rachel thought, *I'll make her some schnitzels*. Dear God, you would not believe how delicious Rachel's schnitzels were: the meat tender, airy, as if prepared on fumes, yet lightly fried, coated with a crispy layer of breadcrumbs, and special eggs possessing light-brown shells and bleeding yolks the color of a Mediterranean sun dipping into the sea. Such eggs were brought from the Poltava region to Kiev, to the Zhitnii Market in the Podil Neighborhood...

What am I talking about? You have probably never even been to Kiev, to the Podil Neighborhood, on Konstantinovsky Street, where Rachel used to live once. And this means you have never been fortunate enough to taste her calves' foot jelly, or stuffed chicken necks, beans cooked in a soup, crushed and mixed with fried onion and goose fat, or the most Jewish of all soups, the "Golden-Yoch"—the highlight of culinary arts, which, beyond its nutritional value, also serves a delightful aesthetic experience: looking at the plate, you see a small lake made of brilliant liquid gold, with enchanting ripples of fat floating on its surface, and pearls of rice scattered in the bottom. And, of course, there's her famous gefilte fish, about which I had better write as few words as possible, for no words could ever do it justice.

A day before her trip to Jerusalem, Rachel went from Bat Yam—the white city hovering over the Mediterranean, where she lived in a small housing project—to the Carmel Market in Tel Aviv. And there—just like once, at the Zhitnii Market in the Podil Neighborhood, elderly farmers from the nearby villages, their heads wrapped with large wool kerchiefs, would fondly say:

"Madam, madam, get your eggs here, fresh from under the chicken's belly, still warm…"—there, in the Carmel Market, strong-armed merchants, hairy and with proud hawkish noses, screamed in the ancient Biblical language, in a virtuosic modulation of throaty sounds: "Three for ten, three for ten!"; "Fresh, fresh, fresh,"; "Watermelon, get your seedless watermelon!"

Rachel immediately headed to the meat stalls, to Itzik, the same regular butcher from whom she would always buy turkey breast, renowned for its quality, daily brought before sunrise from the kibbutzim in the Upper Galilee—fresh, pink. This turkey breast, resting in the transparent refrigerated display stall made of glass and metal and sparkling, spotless clean, looked like a Dutch still-life painting against the snow-white background of Itzik's apron. In the neighboring stalls, meat was dismembered, bones were sawed, poultry was cleaned, and their guts tossed into crates. A still, heavy stench stood in the air, suspended by the blazing forty-degree Celsius temperatures, which could choke you like a gas attack. Inside the poultry guts, large, green flies roamed and settled, and the occasional stray dog would snatch some guts that had already rotted, or a chicken leg, then quickly escape, though no one had noticed it.

It seemed that all this stench and filth had miraculously skipped Itzik's market stall: a piece of ice swollen with snow, glowing in the midst of a tumultuous spring river. Itzik himself looked much like a white bunny that was rescued from flooding, and whose winter fur was yet to change into his summery one.

Rachel took long moments to sort the best of the best. She smelled the meat, pressed it with her finger, and checked how soon her imprinted marks vanished, and which color the created depression had: pale pink meant that the meat was bloodless, one hundred percent kosher, but tasteless and dry; and if it possessed a reddish hue, it meant that a certain amount of blood remained in it after all, and it would froth and sizzle on the skillet, giving the schnitzels life, breath, and juices.

Finally, the best cut was chosen. Rachel paid and exchanged a few sentences in Yiddish with Itzik. Her mastery of that language equaled that she had in the culinary arts. Hers was a Yiddish of milk and honey—"that jargon," as Sholem Aleichem had called it with devious irony. Yes, sure, a jargon—but if so, how could Yiddish have cultivated from its roots a genius with the stature of Sholem Aleichem himself? How could Bashevis Singer have soared on its linguistic wings? But, on the other hand, one must admit that the foundation of classic Yiddish was truly the spoken language, or jargon, of the common people in the towns and villages—all the slaughterers, tailors, and cobblers—speech woven with witticisms and clever words, adorned with sharp humor and bitter, lyrical sadness. From it also emanated the wondrous Chasidic wisdom, Sholem Aleichem's rare humor, and Bashevis Singer's shadowy philosophy. Yes, yes, you can hear from Rachel Fidelman's lips that same pure Yiddish, without additions, the townspeople's Yiddish, which had provided the urge and push that drove all the great Yiddish authors.

Her "R" is a delight to hear. It vibrated in the throat's cavity like a ball dancing inside a blown whistle. (The genuine Jewish R is very rich in its pallet of colors, unlike the cold, dry German R, that sounds like a needle scratching copper, or the blurry French R, losing its inner intensity in the nasal pitch.) The melodic nature of Rachel's Yiddish is achieved by the ups and downs of her intonation, which, like in a roller coaster, coils and curves at the end of each sentence with typical Jewish cunning. And this creates the accent antisemites of all shades of the linguistic spectrum are in the habit of mockingly imitating left and right…

Additionally, Rachel bought her recovering sister chocolate-coated marshmallows, pears, apples, and a jar of honey, just in case dear Sofa ran a fever. The shopping cart was fairly heavy—how will she get it up on the bus? And after all, Rachel is nearly seventy-six years old, though looking at her, you would not be able to tell: a strong woman with smooth facial skin, kindly eyes, and a thin, straight nose that is a literal work of art (reminiscent of a relief made by the great Benvenuto Cellini's hands).

In the tiny kitchen, on the tiny marble table, Rachel cut the turkey breast: she divided it into straight slices, then pounded each slice with a special hammer she had brought from Kiev. Then she began the real work of witchcraft: she spread each slice with spices, according to a recipe known to her alone, dipped them in whipped eggs and breadcrumbs, then lit the stove flame at just the right level. She poured sunflower oil into the skillet and tossed a cube of butter inside: the former contributes to the fried meat's elasticity, the latter helps make it airy. She placed the schnitzels in the skillet, closed it with the cover, and pressed it shut. While the schnitzels were fried, Rachel occasionally lowered the stove flame. A heavenly smell gradually spread in the apartment. Rachel placed the ready schnitzels in a pot, wrapped it with a towel, and placed it in a bag—dear Sofa had to have her schnitzels warm. How naïve: how could the heat be maintained through the night, then through the long bus ride to Jerusalem?

The next morning, Rachel got up early—she had a long way ahead of her. *I'll take bus line forty-six*, she thought. *First, I'll get to the Tel Aviv Central Bus Station, and from there, I'll take a bus to Jerusalem.*

Unlike many immigrants who were not very young, Rachel was not concerned about being unable to manage without Hebrew: someone was bound to help her in the street, if not in Russian than in Yiddish. But at the same time, Rachel noticed how the elderly, perhaps Jews from Poland or Romania, who replied to her in Yiddish, be it at the doctor's office, the grocery store, or on the bus, would lower their voice while speaking, sneaking suspicious sideways glances. Just like in Kiev when Rachel would speak to her mother, who hardly knew Russian, while they sat on a bench in the park. But there, in Kiev, Yiddish had been persecuted, and here? Here, it had simply been pushed aside.

Everything is perfect in the Hebrew language, the queen of all languages. But it isn't very friendly—and is mainly rough towards that Yiddish, who outrageously tries to shove her way into the divine language's family. But how is it possible to deny the great European culture, a whole galaxy created in Yiddish? What is to be done with the rich world of noble masses written about philosophy and religion, with the ingenious literature, the poetry, and theater? Should all of this simply be abandoned like a shipwreck, on the bottom of history's seas, where everything is covered by the residues of forgetfulness? Oh, my poor language, whose entire restless life had been persecuted by both your friends and enemies! No one would ever be able to bring you down – where are they now, eh? All those persecutors? And you, not only are you still alive, but you remain young, clever, and supple…

All the entrances and exits from the Tel Aviv Central Bus Station were secured by soldiers, males and females—two days before, terrorists had blown up a city bus in Jerusalem. Inside, it was unbearably crowded. Rachel stood lost, inside the crowd, turning her silver-crowned head right and left. Along came a corpulent young man, a yarmulke resting on his black, curly hair.

"Excuse me, where is the bus to Jerusalem?"

The young man recoiled from her, as if Rachel were a demon.

"Hebrew, only Hebrew…" he muttered while rushing away.

Rachel was also ignored by two soldiers, whose M-16 rifles' straps crossed over their breasts like the straps of arrow quivers had once crossed the breasts of the ancient Amazons. The ones who finally helped her were several Chassidic men, who, in their appearance, echoed the protagonists of a Jewish Broadway musical: tall, round hats with edges made of fur, *bekishe* frock coats with a cut that meticulously tightened around the waist, knickerbockers, and socks.

"Yes, sweetheart, of course we know," the eldest of them said.

"We know, we know," the others nodded simultaneously.

Oh, what delight they took in Rachel's Yiddish—savory, meaty, authentic. For them, the Chassidim, there were no linguistic dilemmas: that was a holy language.

"Go up, dear, to the sixth floor, using the escalators. Platform No. 36—there's a bus there bound for Jerusalem. And hurry up—it leaves in ten minutes."

The Chassidim rolled on, clumsily waving their arms while loudly, without caring about anyone or anything, speaking in Yiddish. But no one seemed to care: people in Israel have long gotten used to the Chassidim...

A double-decker intercity bus clumsily freed itself from among the narrow streets of South Tel Aviv. Rachel sat at the rear end of the upper level, by the large window, her shopping cart pressed against her legs. She napped. Her head peeked like a silver float over the tall backrest, occasionally disappearing from sight as if sinking underwater.

But when the bus finally broke free of the Tel Aviv overcrowdedness and, like a rare, red bird, started flying towards Jerusalem, Rachel woke and from the bird's view started watching the rapidly changing landscape. In fact, the landscape was fairly monotonous: various hills and ragged, dreary ravines, almost stripped bare of any bushes, yet scattered with small and large stones. Rachel's heart pounded. If you had asked her why, she couldn't have explained it to you. Perhaps she felt that these views did not belong to the earth at all: where else could such views be seen? Thin trickles of copper dripping from above, frozen skies imprisoned in blue ice? Where else could you feel eternity's breeze, vanishing in the optical illusions of the air that's growing tired among these lifeless hills?

At the entrance to Jerusalem, the bus stopped at an army checkpoint. Three burly soldiers, bravehearted Israeli fighters, inspected everything coming or going in or out of the Jewish state's capital. With them was a large dog, a German Shepherd. The bus door opened, and the dog rushed inside. The soldiers rushed in after it, grabbing their rifles. The dog sniffed every object, person, and seat on the bus. In the lower deck—nothing. All was fine. They got up to the upper deck, and there, the dog began to act strangely. Without taking heed of anyone, the dog hurtled on, pulling on its leash, all the way to the last row. It went straight to Rachel, howled, started scratching her shopping cart, and finally placed its head on it, its large tongue lolling and dripping with drool. Rachel panicked. Then the soldiers, following the dog, rushed to her as well.

"What do you have in your cart, ma'am?" the commanding officer asked.

But what was he saying? Who would help poor Rachel? All the other upper deck passengers seemed to have evaporated.

"I am going to my sister, to the hospital. This is for her—there are schnitzels in it, apples, honey..." Rachel said in Yiddish and in Russian.

The soldiers did not understand a single thing. They looked around, but no one was there: everyone had escaped, terrified of a potential bombing.

"Ma'am, you need to come with us now!"

The soldiers tried to pull Rachel by the arm, while she kept saying:

"Dear Sofa had heart surgery, and there is food in the bag for her... honey, apples, pears, schnitzels..."

"Please come with us!" the officer demanded more firmly.

Rachel thought the soldiers had asked her to take out the content of her shopping cart. She began taking out of it bags with fruits, honey, and finally—the towel-wrapped pot with the schnitzels that had already cooled. She removed the blanket, opened the lid to show them what was inside the pot, and even took out one schnitzel and displayed it to them. The dog, who had been closely following Rachel, pounced, grabbed the schnitzel, and instantly swallowed it. How could such a thing have happened? The soldiers stood in utter shock. After all, this was not just any dog, but Nehoshtan—the finest, smartest dog of the elitist IDF's canine unit. It had undergone a highly complicated training process. Nehoshtan had been trained in rescuing injured from the battlefield, neutralizing armed terrorists, identifying drugs, and explosives. Surely, such a highly trained dog would never grab anything from a stranger's hand. Rachel's schnitzels, whose scent that cunning, clever creature had sniffed the moment it had set paw on the bus, stained Nehoshtan's tough and mighty image for many years to come.

The driver's voice rose from below.

"What's the problem?"

"Nothing, everything is fine," the soldiers replied while going down the stairs leading back to the lower deck.

At the Hadassah Ein Kerem Hospital, it was easier: they spoke English there, Russian, even Yiddish. Rachel was directed to some long passageway, connecting two large hospital buildings. Then she went up a staircase, then down an elevator until finally, she found herself in a dark and seemingly endless corridor with large ventilation pipes across its concrete walls. It gave the impression of being a shelter. At the end of the corridor, behind a green door, was the emergency room. The beds were equipped with highly sophisticated machinery. Dear Sofa lay there, hooked up to an infusion, tubes attached to her mouth and nose. Over her head was a monitor, on which the choking lifeline crawled in panic. The ivory-hued skin of her face was completely pale, her eyes shut.

Rachel sat beside her sister. She held dear Sofa's drooped arm— slender, white, with shades of yellow. She spent long moments looking at Sofa's bony face, swayed in sorrowful motions then began to cry. Suddenly, she remembered her shopping cart, jumped to her feet and started taking our bags with fruits, a honey jar, marshmallow— and placed them on the bedside cabinet. A nurse came to Rachel, sniffed deeply, and when she felt the smell of meat, firmly said:

"You can leave the fruits, but fried meat is strictly forbidden for this patient. Take it away!"

If, during the afternoon of the Israeli siesta, one would have looked down at the Jerusalemite Hadassah Ein Kerem hospital, which resembles a vast white ship, he would have noticed one tiny dot detaching from it: Rachel, with her shopping cart. And if he would have looked even more closely, then... but actually, he knows it all already. The dot slowly hovered in the scalding heat of the molten hospital square, then was swallowed into the eternal city's womb.

The Notebook

I am convinced that I will get to heaven. I'm sure you'll ask me, "What makes you so confident?" Well, my confidence is based on the life of righteousness I have been leading these twenty-five years, from the moment I arrived in Israel. Yes, the righteous are the ones who would reach heaven. All that's left is to find out just who these righteous are, and whether I am numbered among them.

The righteous have a special soul. As everyone knows, the human soul is divided into two parts: one is bestial, the other—divine. That other part is what gives a man the image of God. The stronger part of a man's soul—whether the bestial or the divine—is the one that determines his character. If the bestial part is more powerful, then a wave of negative traits drowns the man: jealousy, deceit, cunning, evil, power-mongering, condescension, rudeness, obstinacy, callousness, sadism, etc. If the divine, Godly part is more dominant in a person's soul, we will see before us a man who is wise, polite, cultured, patient, and attentive—and mainly, from his soul, there emanates the light of love for others and for our little brothers, the animals.

But the righteous themselves are divided into two parts. The first one can be called ethical geniuses. They have received, as a gift from God, an utterly righteous soul, without a shred of bestiality in it. They are constantly occupied with doing good for good's sake and for no other objective. Their love depends on nothing. It heals the wounds of the souls of those who need healing and raises a desire to live among those who have lost all hope. There have been few of them in human history. They are called saints. Among the better-known of them, one can mention Moses, Jesus, Buddha, and Saint Francis of Assisi.

The righteous of the other type seem to have formed their righteousness with their own hands. They once had an ordinary soul, in which one part or another had the upper hand. But at the same time, they were blessed with a unique skill: the ability to understand and become deeply familiar with their souls, or—as Socrates had said—with themselves. A distinct example of a righteous man of this second type is Saint Augustine, who lived in 354-430. In his renowned autobiographical book, *Confessions*, in which he describes his life and process of joining the bosom of Christianity, Augustine reveals that until the age of thirty, he had led a promiscuous lifestyle: drank too much, frequented brothels, and sinned in many other ways. At the age of thirty, miraculously, he had sobered up. The blessing of God, as he tells it, had landed on his head. He had turned from a pagan into a Christian, and thanks to his brilliant analytical mind, he penned a series of religious-philosophical books which, along with the works of other religious thinkers, the founders of the church, laid the foundations of the Christian Catholic religion.

When I read *Confessions,* I was very interested to discover how Augustine had been able to rid himself of the sinning—in other words, the bestial—aspect of his soul. It was a highly complicated and agonizing process, and Augustine described it with great skill. But the main thing I was able to learn from this wonderful book is the insight that if you were not born an ethical genius, possessing a righteous soul, but merely arrived at the realization that you must rid yourself of your bestial aspect, then you must struggle to achieve that goal every single day. The second you let down your moral and ethical efforts, even just a little, you soon find yourself slipping down the moral slippery slope, straight into the clutches of bestial instincts.

There is also a weapon for fighting this war: constantly reading the words of the wise. Their written thoughts expand your awareness and your heart, providing wings for your soul and allowing it to hover in ethics' shining beams of light. The wise heal from despair and pessimism. They gift the soul with powers that beget the courage to go on living. I find myself returning time and again to the writings of the ancient Roman thinkings of the Stoic school: Seneca, Epictetus, Marcus Aurelius; the French thinkers: Michel de Montaigne and Blaise Pascal; and our very own Baruch Spinoza. I have been taught many things by Rabbi Nachman of Breslov, for example: "Train yourself to have only good thoughts. They will create miracles in your mind." And I tried to! But I was not up to the task. For several minutes, I thought only of lofty things: about a great person, a brilliant idea, the beauty of creation, or an ingenious work of art. I thought only good things about people and the nature of man. Gripped by moral enthusiasm, I found myself changing the famous Latin phrase: "Of the dead, nothing but good is to be said!" My version, "Of the living, just as of the dead, nothing but good is to be said!"

Yet still, good thoughts last only for a few minutes. Then some person comes by, and you can tell he is a bastard just by looking at him. And you think to yourself: *Here he comes, that miserable bastard!* That negative thought brings other negative thoughts in its train. You remember that this other person is crude, vulgar, and that he often mocks and humiliates you. But you do not say a single thing about him and refuse even to mention his name. He is wiped off your consciousness, your memory. And here, another particularly virtuosic trick is at work: dematerializing a negative phenomenon that actually exists in nature but ceases from existing for you alone.

In short, after a fairly lengthy time of self-work, I began to notice that the number of negative thoughts I was having considerably decreased. On the other hand, the divine part of my soul grew larger. I was getting closer to crossing the line beyond which a good man becomes a righteous one. This meant a genuine opportunity for me to enter heaven's gates was forming.

Now, let us imagine that I indeed am getting there. The road leading to heaven is known to mortals, or at least that is what we imagine. It is known from the intuitive understanding once possessed by the great painters, poets, and genius authors who painted or described in their words how they viewed this imagined reality—the road to heaven. It is also known from the stories of people who have had near-death experiences.

First, the soul separates from the body, which is no longer alive. It flies through a kind of tunnel connecting this world with the next. This tunnel is filled with powerful, lofty light, bearing the soul upward. If skillful doctors are able to overcome the patient's clinical death, then the soul returns to the body, and the person remembers only the brilliant, blinding light.

Those souls whom the tunnel leads to the next world and are intended to reach heaven, stop before heaven's gates. If any of you wishes to see what the gates of heaven look like, you are invited to come visit the lobby of the building where I work as a guard. The same pillars of light, the same amazing energy that fills people's hearts. This is where the muse comes to. Where the souls of the wisest, most righteous arrive. After all, if that were not the case, where would these thoughts I am putting to paper in my notebook this very moment, sitting in that very lobby, be coming from? I cannot possibly be thinking this way independently.

In heaven, they offer me a place to stay: a small tree. Not far from there, larger trees grow, between whose branches flutter the souls of Homer, Shakespeare, and Goethe. The concept of time simply vanishes, replaced by perpetual pleasure. Unlike those who have reached hell and are tormented among the flames, being burned in bonfires or roasted in giant skillets, I myself take pleasure and am able to observe cosmic expanses billions of kilometers wide. But what interests me mostly, obviously, is whatever has to do with the Earth. And now, my gaze chances to land on London. A certain luxury hotel, in the Victorian style. An ornate conference hall. What is that? A Sotheby auction! In the hall, there sit the rich and powerful—men enshrouded in the smoke of Havana cigars, women whiffing of expensive French perfumes. The furs of many rare animals rest upon many of the women's shoulders—chinchillas and sables. On the stand, item No. 27. From my far-off heaven, I strain

my eyes to see what transpires there. Could it be? A pink school
notebook of just twelve pages, in which I once wrote my first short
story in Israel, "Broom." The starting price: ten thousand dollars.
The auctioneer cries: "Ten thousand dollars going once!" A hand
rises from the audience and motions: "Twelve thousand..."

Now, bodiless, sitting on a branch of one of heaven's trees, I distinctly remember the time in which I wrote my first story. I cannot,
even with my mind's eye, relive that deep pain that had gripped my
soul then, a pain that nearly caused me to leave this world. I felt
sick to my stomach due to the reality of Israeli immigration. And
if I hadn't spilled that pain onto the pages of that pink, thin, school
notebook, I'd have left this world long before turning into a righteous man. By the way, this notebook, hailing from the Soviet era,
had cost me two kopeks, or two cents, or two Israeli agorot.

I continue to follow the Sotheby auction, which takes place in
the lavish hotel hall in London. The notebook's price has risen to
thirty thousand dollars.

I had written before about my first story and how I had created
it. Perhaps some will accuse me of repeating myself. If they do, I
have saved a clever sentence from Blaise Pascal for my accusers: "Let
no one accuse me of not saying anything new. The innovation lies in
the placement of the materials."

Now I will tell you something about "Broom" in a different
way, in accordance with my new perspective from this heaven. That
pain that preceded the writing of that story—I could not possibly
describe it. There are too many colors missing in my meager palette
of words. What I can describe, though, is my own view of the first
story I had ever written—a view that had caused deep disappointment and a lack of confidence in my skills and abilities.

Even before I came to Israel, I had written quite a few texts: arti-
cles about the history of Russian and world art, ethical, philosophical masses. But that did not mean I would one day be able to sit and
write an artistic creation—a short story or novella. These are entirely
different tasks. I will not speak here about the essence of the short

story as a genre, and about what is necessary to create it, almost like a sculpted portrait. Nor about the idea, content, composition, or style. When I worked as a laborer and gardener at the military cemetery in Holon, and one day, during my break, I sat on the green grass growing around the soldiers' graves, I did not think about all these things that combine to form a story's structure. All I wanted was one thing: to write to silence my mental anguish. I could not have imagined how difficult it would be to do that. But still, I wrote the story—and I humbly bow before my own willpower.

In those days, when I reread it, I felt very disappointed with myself. Today, out of this heavenly delight, I understand why. It all had to do with the method I used to work on the story. I had spent a very long time searching for the beginning, the first sentence, realizing this was the musical key to the entire creation; according to which my entire text would resonate. I wrote and erased, wrote and erased. And then, when I finally found the first words, it turned out that finding the next ones was not easier. When I finished, I kept polishing and polishing, erasing and adding. And slowly, after reading and correcting the story many times, the words began to fade and tatter. The colors of the thoughts had paled. Their originality had gone. A new pain was added: I had thought that I had talent, and reality came and slapped me into wakefulness.

I do not know how I had been able to gather strength, but I typed up "Broom" and sent it to... America, to a Russian-language newspaper. The most important thing was overcoming myself, as I had nothing to lose on any other aspect. The worst that could happen was they'd write and tell me the story wasn't good, which I already knew myself. Or they wouldn't reply at all. But they did reply! They wrote me that the story is beautiful. They praised the protagonist's powerful character, the eloquent language, and even the writer's intellect, which meant—my own. They finished the letter by saying they would publish the story and asked that I send them more.

I received a similar letter from Germany. Then from Moscow, Kiev, Odessa. Even Israeli newspapers in the Russian language published my first story, "Broom." Then it was translated into Hebrew and fell into the hands of one of Israel's most gifted editors. He published it in the *Haaretz* newspaper, and my literary fate changed completely and took a positive turn.

But what is going on down there, with the auction? Just take a look: the amount has soared to one hundred and twenty thousand dollars! And I thought no one would pay more than fifty thousand. That was also what I told my son, Alex, after sharing the idea about the story yet to be written. He answered me: "Dad, they will pay for this story one hundred and twenty thousand dollars exactly!" And indeed they paid. The hammer strikes. "Sold!" the auctioneer announces. But who has bought it? A Japanese man who prefers to remain anonymous. It seems that he, too, has read this story. So, it seems that this story, and others of mine, were translated into Japanese? Yes indeed. After all, the Japanese live on an island and very much admire poetic and miniature literary forms. Haiku, Tanaka. Stories, novellas. Kawabata… Akutagawa.

Two Sins

A Russian Jew comes to Israel—a small, yet proud country. But the very fact of his Judaism is still being shoved down his throat as it has always been. Or perhaps he is wrong and it has just been turned upside-down, twisted a hundred and eighty degrees so it is still applying painful pressure in the very same places—just on opposite edges.

For example, a Rabbi approaches the Jewish Russian. He has a long, silvery beard like Karl Marx's, and is dressed in a traditional *bekishe* frock coat that has a velvet collar liberally sprinkled with dandruff. His hands are white and smooth, and it is apparent they have never held anything heavier than a single glass, let alone a hammer or the firm weight of an axe.

The Rabbi asks, "Russian, Russian, are you Jewish?"

The Jewish Russian, instead of verbally dispatching that Rabbi to some dubious place where the sun does not shine, erupts into long, convoluted explanations in the manner so typical of his deep soul. He claims that if he wasn't Jewish, he would not even be here, in Israel, in the first place, and so on. And it is a shame that the Jewish Russian is upset. However, the pleased Rabbi has achieved his objective. He rolls away, like a ball, gloating.

But the rage the Jewish Russian is feeling towards the Rabbi is unjustified. In a sense, the Rabbi is right. In reality, the Jewish Russian is not entirely Jewish—or at least, not to the highest level of Jewishness it is possible to attain. In fact, the Russian habitually commits two sins. He eats pork, and, unusually, is not circumcised.

Let us ponder these sins.

Regarding the first; how could anyone not hungrily consume this tasty little piggy? Anyone familiar with its qualities, could they hold back? Wouldn't they have sunk their sharp fangs into the soft, tender meat that beckons with its noble, amber succulence? And how could anyone not succumb to the dizzy spell generated by the divine scent that is so unique? Yes, my friends, the same scent that emanates from the dripping cut, wrapped in pinkish-silvery fat. Or perhaps pork skewers marinated in wine and adorned with onion rings? Or with potatoes mashed into a mouthwatering puree, with fat, sauerkraut, and a bumpy-skinned pickle. And then, of course, have it washed down with a glass of something. The clear glass sweating with impatience.

Apologies, but is this what is called sin?

And as for the circumcision, here's the thing. Any male who hurries to sever their foreskin so as to get closer to the Biblical People's tradition, ultimately comes across a rather surprising development. Their wives—who, by the way, are Jewish Russian women—in the sweetest of moments, if we might call it that, suddenly turn their backs on their menfolk, turning away all the prettiest parts of them. Yes, of course there are explanations, hollow all. One time they might say they are tired, another time sick. In fact, they are recalling, with longing it must be said, that very same mythical foreskin that has now been denied to them.

And in their hearts, those damnable women are saying, "You will get nothing from me, you idiot! Why? Because I cannot get the same satisfaction from you as I did before."

And he, the stallion, oh, what a stallion! All of him is left gasping with unfulfilled lust! But the Jewish Russian woman? Well, she may be a gentle soul, but is still as stubborn as they get. Touching her with bare hands may still be possible, but to take her by force? No, that is out of the question!

Before long, the facts are shared with the press who begin to make some noise. It is as if it isn't enough that doctors and musicians cannot get jobs in their professions, let alone buy their own apartments. Now the sexual assimilation of Russian immigrants into society has also failed.

Therefore, there is only one conclusion to be drawn, the action necessary is clear—steer clear of Rabbis, and keep your foreskins with you if you do not absolutely have to sacrifice them. One journalist, a wisecracker, finished his article about the subject with a poem. Short, and very dirty:

One dark, cold night Delilah snuck
And the poor guy's head she plucked.
There are no idiots in this nation
Don't make your organ a donation!

Obviously, Judith, who cut off Holofernes' head, has been replaced here by Delilah. This is all well and good, but the Dweller in the Skies is angry. On the other hand—the devil is rubbing his hands with enjoyment, '*Yes, yes, fresh human meat!*' And he goes ahead and reserves places in the lowest circles of hell. And there, my friends, cauldrons are bubbling with the rosin boiling in them, and there the scorching pans sizzle. And above all can be heard the insufferable cries of sinners. But who will hear them? Who will ease their suffering? Certainly not the hoofed, tailed, horned ones who gleefully stoke the fires…

Miata
A Tel Aviv Fairy Tale

Once upon a time there was a Miata, a small Japanese car. Its fine beauty was often compared to Matsuo Basho's haiku:

"Butterfly wings
Woke the forest clearing
To meet the rising sun."

In its lightness and sublime simplicity, it reminded the Japanese of their Japan. The fate of the Miata had been decided even before its birth. It would sail on a white ship with numerous decks, across oceans and seas, to go and live... where? America? Europe? Or would it end up on the same Asian continent it had been born on? Exactly, in Asia!

When the ship entered the Sea of Japan and began to drift away from the shores of the country, it was not sadness that glimmered in Miata's eyes. No, this was exactly the reason for which it had been born—to reveal to the world Japanese genius.

The ship's destination was Israel. A small and mysterious country, enshrouded in the mists of myths and legends. A country greatly admired in Japan. For how could one gifted people not respect another?

Miata felt good between her brothers and sisters—Hondas, Toyotas, Suzukis and Nissans. And they, their designs lacking any aristocratic finesse, gazed upon her in awe. Especially when the first sunbeams shimmered over the horizon, gently stroking her with their golden light. For all those cars knew how to appreciate Miata's beauty, even though they also had a very fine opinion of themselves. Having been created in Japan, they knew their true value well.

In one of Israel's ports, Miata received a royal welcome. They brought transportation for her and she made her way to her lavish new dwelling place in the city of Tel Aviv. There, Miata was provided with a special place, a regal throne in a luxurious showroom, gleaming under the many lights.

One day a real prince came to the showroom. He was tall and had blue eyes, a ginger beard and locks of bronze. The prince looked like one of Homer's heroes of mythology. Needless to say he was possessed of refined artistic taste. It took just a single glance at Miata for him to understand it all. Miata's body radiated harmony. The delicate combination of all her parts, the magnificent plasticity and perfection of proportion, the marvelous skill with which such a technical feat had been accomplished, all combined to make Miata an aesthetic phenomenon. A genuine work of art.

And her color! Such a divine color! The depth and complexity could never be conceived of in mundane terms. But the connoisseur prince, pursuing unique adventures in color, immediately solved with his gaze, a gaze that could never be sated, the most complicated of coloristic riddles. Here, he saw a rare light, silvery, nearly invisible. Created in one particular moment, a specific instant, on the borderline where two dimensions met… when, at sundown, the fading light blue of the sky gently touched the black cloak that sprawled over the night, in the same way the seagull touches the blue of the sea with its wing.

With the prince, Miata left the regal showroom for his palace situated on the shores of a warm, blue sea, the sea where European civilization, with which Miata was not yet familiar, had been born.

The prince introduced Miata to the white, magical city, hovering like a rare bird over the sea. Miata loved it all; the wide, spacious boulevards awash with blinding, southern sunbeams; and the people bathing in the blue ocean, moving like seagulls on the low waves.

The people! Oh, those people! Descendants of the people who had created the ancient civilization Miata now gazed upon in awe. Simple people, happy, open and intelligent. The prince loved beautiful Miata with all his heart. And she simply worshipped him. But then, one day...

...and here one event or another is supposed to happen, preferably a tragic one, around which fairy tales could be written. In Little Red Riding Hood, for example, the wolf devours the grandma, then the hunters kill the wolf. If this logic was to be followed, something should now happen to Miata. For example, she could be stolen by evil people, taken to a remote village and dismantled for parts. And the prince? No, I will not speak more of him—so as to not go asking for trouble. Why? Because the prince's character has been based on that of my own son. And Miata is in his possession to this very day, delighting every eye that chances to fall on her with her perfect shape and form.

Matzah

"A German, by nature, is a kind-hearted and generous person. He does not want to see human beings humiliated."

— Johann Wolfgang von Goethe, *From my Life: Poetry and Truth*

On Passover Eve, in the rotation department of a printing house of the country's major newspaper, the offset machine broke down. It was the same machine that was often called *"the alcoholic old lady,"* a dubious tribute to the countless barrels of alcohol she had consumed in the twelve years of her activity. It was alcohol necessary to get just the right level of thickness in the desired color of printing. Every half hour, the old lady sucked in and devoured a giant Swedish, or Norwegian, roll of paper weighing 1,200 kilograms. Numerous wheels and cylinders spun at insane speeds in the bowels of the machine, their perfect bodies impregnated by the touch of the paper, color and alcohol. Five times a week the machine would give birth to all the editions of the newspaper, including the supplements.

The part that had broken was the piece that was responsible for the final stage of the "birthing," the stage that, in normal operating times, was supposed to forcibly thrust the bound issues, on a conveyor belt, into the outside world. The machine was German manufactured, and to fix it, two Germans from Munich had been summoned. The older of the two looked kindhearted. He was tall, with a white mustache and beard, and resembled Santa Claus in his appearance. The bright pinkish color of his bald spot stood out in stark contrast with the gray background of the printing department.

51

The younger German looked more like an athlete. He had a shapely body, and the sense of youthful strength he exuded seemed to give him a constant smile that perpetually sprouted beneath his lush mustache, reminiscent of Nietzsche's.

The two Germans worked efficiently, and all who came to observe their work witnessed firsthand that the legendary efficiency of German laborers was no invention. Their working environment was organized in exemplary fashion, their work tools were varied and laid out to be user-friendly, and the way they moved was measured, solid, calculated, harmonious and efficient.

Toward noon, the Germans had tired. Their jokes, woven into their musical south-German dialect, became more restrained, and their laughter short-lived and fragmented. At noon exactly, they sat down at the dining table right there, in the department. But, because there is no bread in Israel during Passover, only *matzah*, the Germans had to put their juicy slice of Bavarian sausage, with its delicate layer of white-bluish fat at the edges, between two dry, cardboard-like pieces of flatbread *matzah*. The *matzah* obediently crumbled under their sharp, healthy, German teeth, before being dampened by the moist air of velvety canned beer, and sinking into the infinite darkness of the German stomachs…

I had nothing against the desire of those life-craving Germans to eat pastrami *matzah* sandwiches for lunch, but there was something—just a little something—that pinched my heart. And the resemblance suddenly began to create, in the heavy, cubistic-like air rife with the fumes of colors, a transparent image of Kyiv at the end of September 1941. One of the many images of that war that had been etched into my memory by my grandfather's stories.

In the soft days of autumn, redolent with golden leaves that had already fallen, and the chocolate-dark chestnuts that blanketed the boulevards, everyone had urgently fled the city, and my grandfather had missed the last trains offering escape. And when he crossed the Dnieper towards Darnytskyi on an old chain bridge that was about to be blown at any moment, Kyiv's western line of defense broke, and

German tanks rushed headlong into the city, along with the infantry. As much as my grandfather had hurried, the Germans had still caught up with him a few days later. The day before, he had gone to sleep in a haystack. Then the Germans had arrived and, scattering in the field, had checked each stack with a few jabs of their rifle bayonets in several places in each stack. How lucky my grandfather had been. Twice, once in each war, he had stared straight into death's murky gaze. In 1919, in a Jewish town, a Cossack had taken pity on him for some reason, and returned his sword to its scabbard. Then in September 1941, a German bayonet had nearly drowned my grandfather in the cold sweat of mortal fear, not to mention his blood, when it slid past his right ear. The bayonet was withdrawn and then plunged into the stack again, this time passing an inch or two in front of his eyes. Yes, he had been lucky, my grandfather, because he ended up dying at age eighty, in the comfort of his bed…

The vision vanished with the same suddenness with which it had appeared. The Germans had finished eating their sandwiches and had drunk all their beer. Then they sprawled comfortably back in their chairs and lit cigarettes. Itzik, the old maintenance worker, brought them strong, fragrant coffee. After they had finished drinking—which marked the end of the meal—the Germans brushed the *matzah* crumbs off their coveralls and went back to work. The next day, the machine was again gobbling up gigantic rolls of paper and color, was intoxicated with alcohol, and birthed the new edition of the newspaper.

Including the supplements, of course.

Ten Agorot

"I have labored carefully, not to mock, lament, or execrate, but to understand human actions."

— Baruch Spinoza - *Tractatus politicus*

1.

I never would have imagined that a single, ten agorot coin would become one of the main protagonists in my story—but here it is; I'm looking at it right now. It is a metal disk, 2.2 centimeters in diameter and a light bronze in color. On one side is stamped the number "10"—but not randomly. It is carefully placed against the background of a square, and the square is bounded by a circle. The square is wholly comprised of parallel lines that furrow into the coin as if etched by a needle. The texture of the background is what gives the number ten a special, regal quality. If you compare the two number tens, the one on the ten agorot coin, and the one on the ten shekel coin, you will see that the ten on the shekel coin is far inferior to the ten on the agorot. And that is because the round, decidedly unaccomplished background on the shekel seems to emphasize the humiliating size of the zero. On the ten shekel coin, the zero is much smaller than the number one. Why is this? After all, everyone knows for a fact that what allows the lowly valued number ten to become a proud ten, can only be the size of the zero.

On one side of the square, the word *"Agorot"* is written in both English and Hebrew. Under the square is the coin's year of manufacture. On the other side of the coin, the *menorah* is embossed twice, and the word *"Israel"* is written in three languages—Hebrew, Arabic and English. That is all. That is what the smallest, least valuable coin, worth ten agorot, looks like.

As I examine this coin, I indulge in thoughts about the microscopic phenomena of our lives. Who, other than myself, would take such a meticulous interest in a ten agorot coin? Only me, as I have an artistic interest, the coin being a protagonist in my own story. There are many people among us who, quite literally, never even allow the existence of such a coin to enter their consciousness.

The rich, for example.

Let us try to understand their attitude to money. In this context, I remember a particular case in the company where I worked as a guard. One day, the company owner, a man known for his great wealth, summoned me to him. It was a few days before the holiday of *Rosh Hashana*. His intentions were highly admirable. He offered me a one-thousand shekel holiday bonus. He took out a large leather wallet and opened it. In it, I saw an illogically thick wad of two-hundred shekel bills. The wallet looked very heavy, and the wad of bills—dark red in color—reminded me of a Dutch brick that had been processed by fire, and from which the wonders of Dutch architecture had been created. I then thought that should this wallet, this heavy brick, chance to fall on my head in some mysterious way, I might well have suffered a first, or even second-degree concussion.

The question I ask is this: Is a man that rich, like the owner of the company I once worked for as a guard, aware of the existence of ten agorot coins? The answer must be no. For him, a lowly object like that does not exist in nature. Okay, so what about the CEO of the Bank of Israel, or the managers of commercial banks who receive bonuses of a million shekels or more? Perhaps the owners of oil or gas companies have seen or heard something about the ten agorot coin? Unlikely. Contractors, then? Israeli rock stars, or the *Mizrahi* singers who steal one's breath and heart with their magically twirling voices? Or perhaps the singers, the most famous of whom are paid a hundred and fifty to two hundred thousand shekels for staging public shows on Independence Day? No, of course not! All these people have just a vague idea of the existence of the ten agorot coin... that is, if they know about it at all.

So, what is this ten agorot coin? A metaphysical, next to invisible, object, one that cannot be perceived by any self-respecting or rich Israeli. Yes, the fortunate people who possess self-respect or riches are unable to see or notice this coin, while the poor—who, as everyone knows, are possessed of a much reduced self-respect—are very aware of it.

There are even some who deal exclusively in ten agorot coins. Drug addicts, for example, who beg by crossroad traffic lights. In most cases, the coin tossed from an open car window into the begging addict's paper cup is ten agorot. And they would make a decent living from their begging if the owners of the nearby shops and kiosks didn't give them only half the value of the coins when they exchange them for goods.

In this same group can be counted the limping grandmothers who skillfully infiltrate the long rows of cars waiting for the traffic light to turn green. This large group—myriads of pensioners, Holocaust survivors living off a minimum social security allowance—are the ones who count every agora, and pray every day to have enough money to make ends meet.

Finally, there is the largest group of Israeli citizens who cannot be indifferent to this coin: the people who earn minimum wage. I know what I am talking about because I myself am one of them. And our group numbers in the tens of thousands...

I could go on endlessly and detail much more about the rich internal and external life of the ten agorot coin—a coin that is seemingly small and insignificant. But what I have already related here is enough, especially seeing as it is but the introduction to the story of something that happened one morning when my own personal fate became interwoven with the fate of this coin in the most fatal of ways...

2.

I work as a guard in the lobby of a building located at 10 Dubnov Street in Tel Aviv. My shift begins at seven in the morning. At about nine, a stack of the famous daily newspaper *Today* is delivered. It's a paper that is making a lot of waves in Israel, especially as it is distributed free of charge. Whenever I am not thinking about serious matters, I sometimes allow myself to ponder the strange fate of this newspaper. And the more I think about it, the more I am convinced it deserves detailed and highly refined intellectual analysis. Beyond that... well, it sometimes seems to me that the newspaper holds a convoluted logical riddle, one that is far from easy to solve.

What are the details of this riddle? A certain Jewish American billionaire feels much sympathy for a particularly gifted Israeli politician. (I'll call the politician "X," so I can avoid any legal issues and complaints). X's extraordinary gifts as an orator are simply spellbinding to our billionaire. I cannot know this for a fact, but the billionaire might well be assisting the Israeli politician in his election campaigns by offering financial aid—all within the framework allowed by law, of course. After all, everyone knows politician X always meticulously adheres to the rules. But our Jewish American billionaire went a step further, and began working to make his whims become reality.

Those whims are typically harbored by many of the rich, and he decides, by investing a not inconsiderable amount of money, to publish a newspaper that will provide strong ideological support to politician X, whom he appreciates, and to politician X alone. Now, why did I say that the Jewish American billionaire is prone to flights of fancy and whims? Because they are a symptom of strange and unexpected behavior. Obviously, this is a moral defect; a person of considerable fortune, who thinks he can get away with anything, and even gives free rein to his caprices, loses his sensitivity to the interest of society as a whole, and puts his own interests first, harming society in the process.

People might ask me why I claim it is a whim when a Jewish American billionaire publishes a newspaper with his own money—even if the newspaper is personal and tendentious. What harm can such a newspaper cause society? After all, they say the opposite is true, that such a newspaper only contributes to society because it attracts many people who otherwise wouldn't be reading any newspaper at all.

Well, it just isn't that simple. Did this Jewish American billionaire ever stop to consider that by realizing his dream project in the form of publishing and distributing a free newspaper, he was creating a monster? A media *golem* that would eventually destroy the entire newspaper market in Israel and cause the demise of the printed newspaper as we know it? The printed newspaper tradition that has a history stretching back two thousand years in time? In fact, to news announcements made in ancient Rome to update Romans about the various occurrences that were taking place in the city. Scrolls, copied by hand and named *Akta Durnal Populi* (Daily Public Records), like a daily gazette, were hung in public squares and handed to politicians or influential citizens. It was Julius Caesar who instructed that transcripts from Senate meetings, reports from military leaders, and the missives from the leaders of neighboring countries, all be made available to the general citizenry.

The first real printed newspaper in history was *Bulletin of the Court,* published in China in the eighth century. It featured imperial decrees and descriptions of major events. The newspapers were printed using metal plates on which pictograms were engraved. The plates were then coated with ink and the newspapers printed.

The first printed European newspaper was published around 1605 in Strasburg. It was named: *Relation: Aller Fuernemmen und Gedenckwuerdigen Historien.* The editor and publisher was a printer called Johann Carolus, who had previously published handwritten newspapers.

But despite this rich and ancient history, the days of the printed newspaper are numbered. The twentieth century saw the introduction of what would eventually prove to be the printed media's undertaker—the internet. However, as long as generations of people in their sixties, seventies, eighties and older are still alive, so, also, will printed newspapers survive. And if evolution does, in the end, demand their demise, then it should be as natural as the passing of a human being, not an unnatural murder committed by a daily free newspaper.

Such thoughts pervade my mind in the mornings, when, at about nine, copies of the daily edition of *Today* are delivered to the lobby of the building located at 10 Dubnov Street in Tel Aviv, where I work as a guard.

On the security desk, a stack of one hundred copies is placed. Can I, in some way, affect their fate? Can I slow, or even bring to a complete halt, the distribution of this harbinger of the death of printed media? Perhaps I could convince people not to take *Today* because the newspaper is free and therefore of poor quality, convincing them, instead, to buy one of the major newspapers, *Haaretz* or *Yediot*. But that would be a lie, there are some wonderful journalists working for *Today*. Maybe I could take the whole stack of papers off the front desk and toss them in the trash? But that wouldn't help either—about five hundred meters from the building where I sit, on the corner of King Saul Boulevard and Ibn Gabirol Street, at the entrance of a large supermarket, is a distributor wearing red overalls. On his stand are stacked, not a hundred copies, but a thousand. Anyone can pick a copy up there too. There's enough to go around for everyone, and with plenty to spare...

So how could anyone influence this destructive process? At least symbolically, to create the feeling—even an imaginary one—that something is being done to counter the injustice.

And then, suddenly, a heaven-sent, magical idea came to my mind, an idea directly related to the ten agorot coin. I will sell the paper! It will have a price tag—ten agorot! And I will sell it as a sort of joke. Anyone who doesn't want to pay, won't have to. The objective? Donations. The money would be used to buy diapers for nursing homes where the elderly lie motionless.

I recalled the place where my mother spent the final year of her life, and where she had passed. There had always been, for some reason, a shortage of diapers. I made a quick calculation. If I sold all hundred copies of the newspaper, I could make as much as ten shekels a day. But not everyone would have a ten agorot coin. And there would also be some who, out of principle, would refuse to pay. Whatever the case, in a month or two, I would have earned a hundred shekels. Enough for me to buy a box of diapers...

My calculations were soon proven to be correct, even though at first, people were surprised.

"What do you mean? *Today* is no longer a free newspaper?"

I explained, and many nodded in understanding, reaching into their pockets for a ten agorot coin. I handed them the paper. Others claimed that the newspaper was free, they wanted to have it free of charge. I never argued. "There you go," I told them. And they would leave with their free copy.

After about two months I had finally amassed a hundred shekels. I bought a box of diapers, and on my day off—Friday— headed to the nursing home. I walked the same agonizing path I'd once walked every day for a whole year, the last year of my mother's life. And the bitter feelings I'd felt back then, two years earlier, flooded back, threatening to overwhelm me. There, I saw the same three-storied building. First floor, second floor, and then the third—which had been my mother's. Miserable, wheelchair-bound old men and women. Many of those I had known at that time were no longer alive. A heavy, indefinable smell filled the corridor. It was almost impossible to breathe. My heart was filled with hurt, but it wasn't a physical pain. It seemed to be something squeezing my heart, crushing it under the weight of memories, under a burden near impossible to carry. I peeked into the room where my mother had once slept. The bed by the window, where she had lain unmoving for a full year, was empty.

3.

And then, lightning suddenly struck. The day had begun with a charmingly sunny morning, and my mood was appropriately wonderful. The *Today* newspaper sold with great success that day. The pile of ten agorot coins swelled and grew taller. There were many visitors to the building. On the fourth floor was the clinic run by an excellent dentist, Dr. Jacques. The ground floor was occupied by the clinic of the cardiologist, Dr. Bella. On the same floor there was also a talented gynecologist, Dr. Daniel. The flow of women coming to his clinic was unceasing. They all willingly took the newspaper—and paid the ten agorot.

At ten o'clock, an elegantly dressed woman approached my security desk. As will be revealed later on, she was not there to attend gynecologist Dr. Daniel's clinic, nor was she there to see cardiologist Dr. Bella. In fact she had come to keep an appointment at the offices of attorneys Shmulik K and Guy N, which are located on the first floor. I was more familiar with Shmulik K than I was with his partner, Guy N, as we shared a common intellectual interest—the works of Franz Kafka.

The works of the genius from Prague, or to be more precise, his unpublished papers, or, to be even more precise, the legal battle over the ownership of the unpublished papers, was what had made attorney Shmulik K's name a very familiar one. He had been part of an international legal debate that had spanned several years, and had become known as the ultimate expert in the question of ownership involving the inheritors of several of Kafka's novels, short stories, novellas and letters.

Shmulik K was deeply familiar with the works of Kafka. Which was why, whenever he had a moment to spare between seeing clients and participating in court debates, we would talk about the revered writer. Shmulik K analyzed the author's novels and short stories with great sensitivity. He mainly excelled in analyzing *The Trial*, as the manuscript had become one of the most hotly debated issues in the international legal dispute.

Indeed, it was this novel that most accurately represented the main body of Kafka's work. It is based on two things—allegorical thinking typical of prophets, philosophers and genius authors, and the absurd. The high point of *The Trial* is the short parable, "Before the Law," which appears in the ninth chapter of the novel, entitled, "In the Cathedral." As for myself, I have used this universal parable, with all its multifaceted, elusive and slippery meanings, more than once in my own stories.

And it was at that very moment that the lightning struck; that the ending of the parable suddenly made the whole absurd situation clear to me. A situation related to something as simple as the publication of a newspaper in Israel. A publication funded by an American billionaire to support politician X.

The parable begins like this: *"In front of the law there is a doorkeeper. A man from the countryside comes up to the door and asks for entry. But the doorkeeper says he can't let him in to the law right now..."*

The doorkeeper knows he won't ever let the man in, not now, not ever. But he does not say that to the man from the countryside, because the man had not asked him. The man from the countryside waited for the moment to come when he would be admitted through the door to the law. And so he waited by the door for the rest of his life.

Kafka ends the parable like this: *"Now he no longer has much time to live. Before his death he gathers in his head all his experiences of the entire time up into one question which he has not yet put to the gatekeeper. He waves to him, since he can no longer lift up his stiffening body.*

"The gatekeeper has to bend way down to him, for the great difference has changed things to the disadvantage of the man. 'What do you still want to know, then?' asks the gatekeeper. 'You are insatiable.'

"'Everyone strives after the law,' says the man, 'so how is it that in these many years no one except me has requested entry?'

"The gatekeeper sees that the man is already dying and, in order to reach his diminishing sense of hearing, he shouts at him, 'Here no

one else can gain entry, since this entrance was assigned only to you. I'm going now to close it."'

The absurdities that surrounded the *Today* newspaper were a little more complicated than the Kafkaesque door to the law. The newspaper was essentially published for the benefit of one man alone—politician X—but unlike the door of the law, which allowed entry to no one, many thousands could "enter" the newspaper. Its ending, however, will be identical to the one described by Kafka in the parable of *The Trial's* ninth chapter. As soon as X retires from political life, the newspaper, like the door to the law, will close, as it was designed only to assist politician X.

But let us retrace our steps to the elegant woman who approached my security desk at ten in the morning and reached out to take a copy of *Today*. I told her the newspaper cost ten agorot.

"Why?" the lady asked, and the thin line of her stylized eyebrows rose in wonder. "After all, this newspaper is distributed free!"

I explained to her, it was for charity.

"For charity, I can donate more than ten agorot. But demanding money for something that is free… well, that is a felony!"

"But I am not demanding anything!" I tried to justify myself. "I'm merely asking. You can take the paper for free if you want to."

"No, I won't take the paper, nor will I let this story pass unchallenged!"

And indeed she did not.

She filed a police complaint.

4.

From that point on, events unfolded slowly—as everyone knows, the police are never in a hurry to get anywhere. The slow progression of an investigation is the most effective means the police have of putting pressure on a suspect who, much like Kafka's protagonist, Joseph K, is a prisoner in his own solitude, trapped in his own vulnerable mental frame, his own nightmares, and, ultimately finding himself devoid of any strength and lacking any ability to resist, falls like ripe fruit into the waiting hands of the investigators.

Two weeks or so later, a short-statured man appeared in the lobby. He was wearing a faded, wrinkled T-shirt and a pair of ripped jeans. His small skull was clean-shaven. A silver earring glittered in his left earlobe. He stood by the wall, presumably so he would not be noticed. And, indeed, he *was* inconspicuous. I didn't notice him at all, and even if I had—could I have suspected he was a policeman?

The newspaper sold well that morning. People happily paid their ten agorot. The guy with the shaven head and the silver earring stood by the wall taking pictures. That did not bother me in the least. Then he came over to my desk, picked up a newspaper and handed me my ten agorot. A clicking sound came from his cell phone. He thanked me and left the building through the revolving doors. About a month later, another policeman entered the lobby. This time he presented me with an ID and introduced himself.

"Eli, Tel Aviv Police investigator."

He told me they had received a complaint that I was engaging in illegal commerce, or in other words, I had been selling the free *Today* newspaper for ten agorot a copy. My heart skipped a beat. My mouth went dry. Unlike the first policeman, who had been sloppily dressed, and who, I now realized, had documented the process of me selling the newspaper, Eli was elegantly dressed in a short-sleeved striped shirt, edges neatly tucked into a classic pair of jeans. In his right hand he held a dark-brown leather briefcase. His features failed to make an impression and quickly slipped from my memory. Even now, as I am writing these lines, I cannot remember what he looked like. But it was different with his eyes. Steely, metallic gray, they etched themselves into my memory. So much so that they often feature in my nightmares. They gleamed with a powerful, intrusive energy.

As Eli interrogated me, those eyes would occasionally lift off the paper he was writing my replies to his questions on and, for some reason, he would direct his sharp, metallic gaze straight into my left eye. Why did he do that? Maybe it was an interrogation method used by the Tel Aviv Police? Or perhaps he knew I was left-handed, so he thought it would be easier for him to influence my subconscious? No, I don't think so, but still, Eli's gaze pierced right into the marrow of my bones, and cold sweat beaded on my forehead.

Well… back to the moment when Eli introduced himself…

"Eli, Tel Aviv Police investigator."

He arrived in the lobby just before the end of my shift. I finished my work and we went together up to the seventh floor of Beit Amot Mishpat, the building where my boss Shlomo A's office is located. It appeared that Eli had already scheduled to meet with him. Shlomo shook the investigator's hand, bestowed a quick nod on me, and left the office. Eli sat in Shlomo's chair, and I sat opposite him. He took a few pages and a pen from his briefcase and prepared to write.

"Well, speak," Eli said. "Why are you selling a newspaper that is not for sale? What are you hoping to accomplish? To make a profit by charging ten agorot an issue?"

I started to tell Eli about the charity, about the nursing home where my mother had stayed…

Eli cut in.

"How long have you been selling the newspaper?"

"About two months," I replied.

"And how much money have you made?"

"A hundred shekels exactly. When I reached that amount I bought a box of diapers and took it to the nursing home."

"Did you keep the receipt?"

"No!"

Eli carefully wrote down every word I uttered.

"You've been selling the newspaper for two months. Why have you made only a hundred shekels?"

I shrugged. "Not everyone bought it. Some did not have a ten agorot coin. Others, people of principle, like the woman who has filed a complaint against me, refused to pay and I gave them the newspaper for free."

The investigator finished his notes, wrote down the place where the interrogation had taken place, Tel Aviv, and added the date. Then he asked me to sign the protocol. I refused, explaining that my command of Hebrew was not good enough and that it would be better for me if the protocol was translated into Russian.

To that Eli calmly replied, "We can manage just as well without your signature. I hope you won't deny everything you just told me when you're in court."

We went back down to the lobby and left the building. Eli bade me farewell, climbed into a white Toyota, and drove off through the parking lot gate.

A month passed. A month during which I lost my appetite and was barely able to sleep. I would wake at two in the morning, tossing and turning in bed until the dawn light sent its chilly fingers creeping through my window. And all the time I was eating myself up from the inside. My thoughts, dismal and dark, raced in loops and circles, spurred on, like circus horses, by the whip of fear. And in the few moments I was able to sink into a fitful sleep, out of the darkness, casting a beam of blinding, accusing light, Police Investigator Eli's gaze rested on me.

Then I received a summons from the District Court in Tel Aviv. That was it, the circle had closed. What should I do? What could I do? Who would help me? There was only one man who I thought might be able to—Shmulik K. I made an official appointment to see him through his secretary, Soli, a girl of rare beauty echoing that of Andersen's Little Mermaid.

That Wednesday, after I had finished my shift, I went up from the lobby, where I sat for eight hours every day, to the first floor and entered the offices of Attorneys Shmulik K and Guy N. I made my way through a maze of corridors, which reminded me of a gallery as the walls were hung with paintings by Shmulik K's father—a gifted Israeli painter—and walked into the lawyer's office. A huge desk sat by the wall furthest from the door. Shmulik K rose to greet me, moving past the desk, and suggested we sit at a small table near the door.

Some time later Soli quietly came in and placed two espressos on the table.

"I'm listening. What's the story here?" Shmulik K asked.

I told him about everything that had happened, providing more details than I'd given the police. I described not just the facts about the selling of *Today* for ten agorot per copy, the buying of diapers for the elderly in the nursing home, the complaint that had been lodged with the police and the subsequent interrogation, but all the psychological nuances as well. I told him of my feelings and the possible development of the affair, as I understood it.

Shmulik K listened attentively, not interrupting even once. When I finished talking, he sank into thought for a few moments.

"A clear violation of the law exists in your story," he finally said, "but I do not see a crime in it. From a theoretical point of view, a violation of the law differs from a crime only in the quantitative sense. In other words—in the terms of its scope and not in its essence in terms of the harm done to society. And if we base our defense on the principles of high morality, which was what motivated you to act, and paint it with the colors of grace, then we might be able to turn this felony into a false charge—which it truly is, and emerge from court with a verdict of innocent... I hope!"

On the day of the court hearing I arrived at 10 Dubnov Street in Tel Aviv and met Shmulik K in the lobby. Seven minutes were enough for us to travel the five hundred meters along Shaul Hamelech Street to the District Courthouse in Weisman 2. At the entrance, we were searched by the security personnel. The hall the hearing took place in was on the first floor. We marched up a corridor, turned right, and stepped into a small courtroom. It was filled with people. Apparently, as well as my case, several others were to be heard too. My case was first.

At nine o'clock precisely, Judge Deborah Lichtenstein and her stenographer emerged from a side door and entered the courtroom. The judge sat regally behind the bench, picked up the stack of files waiting on it for her, and declared:

"The case of Leonid Pekarovsky."

She gave the floor to the prosecutor who was there to state the case against me on the Israel Police's behalf. The prosecutor rose. Began to speak. He spoke slowly, and it seemed as if he was searching for words he did not have. In a few sentences, he described the essence of the lawsuit, then recounted the counts the prosecution were accusing me of. The first was the illegal sale of goods—the *Today* newspaper, which was not intended for sale, as was clearly stated on its front page. The second was the selling of goods in an unauthorized location during working hours. The third involved tax evasion and failure to report profits made.

"In accordance with the relevant clauses in the law book..." The prosecutor went on to relate them in detail one by one and then came to his closing. "The prosecution asks that the court sentences the defendant, Leonid Pekarovsky, to imprisonment for a period of twelve months, and imposes a fine to be paid to the state treasury in the sum of 300,000 shekels..."

Something happened to me. My head began to spin. My ears echoed with the words, *"Three counts of felony, three counts of felony!"* The Tel Aviv courtroom faded into a blur, and then disappeared completely. I heard, from somewhere, the words once spoken by Jesus in Hebrew, *"You will deny three times that you know me."* And out of the depths of my temporarily destroyed vision, the image of Peter the Apostle, to whom those words had been directed, was suddenly tangible before me...

But other words, also spoken in Hebrew, this time by Judge Deborah Lichtenstein, brought me back to reality.

"The defense will have the floor now."

Shmulik K got slowly to his feet, his stature tall, his juicy baritone voice imbued with a plethora of colorful intonations. His gesticulations were calm and measured and meticulous, and seemed to give more credibility to his every word, thus bolstering the logic in the arguments he was making. The whole effect, set against the background of his intellect, emphasized the artistic skills Shmulik K was blessed with.

I will now deviate from the thread of what happened and skip forward a day after the courtroom debate, when Shmulik K arrived to enter his offices in the building.

I asked him, "Shmulik, how were you able to deliver such a brilliant speech, which was, may I say, a work of art in itself?"

"I carefully and meticulously prepared for this case," Shmulik K answered. "I had to protect you from being convicted. Having had experience with the trial relating to Kafka's literary estate, I knew that, psychologically, my speech had to be so emotional that it would take by storm the emotions of the judge, everyone in the courtroom, and even the prosecutor's. I did not immediately decide which strategy to employ. As you are an author, I refreshed my memory on the history of a few of the most famous trials of the past involving poets and writers—Dostoyevsky, Flaubert, Baudelaire, and Oscar Wilde. But I had to be careful, as their cases were not very similar to yours.

"Then I remembered Cicero's speech, delivered in 62 BC, in defense of the Greek poet, Archias. That speech, one of the Roman orator's most famous, was different from those usually given before the courts because it was 'Epideictic,' or belonging to the genre of ceremonial oratory. The speech was so unusual in the art of ancient Roman oratory that Cicero himself said that he employed, '... *this style of speaking, which is at variance, not only with the ordinary usages of courts of justice, but with the general style of forensic pleading...*' The innovative aspects of this speech had to do with the fact that Cicero emphasized, in a ceremonial (Epideictic) way, the special role that the talented poet, Archias, played in the cultural life of ancient Rome.

"At the same time, and for the first time in a speech given in a court of law, Cicero talked about the virtues of aesthetic education, about the useful benefits that the different arts brought to various aspects of both private and social life. He said literature and music advance thinking, encourage bravery, comfort us in our old age...

"I came to the conclusion that I had to use the psychological principles of Cicero's speech, but instead of aesthetics, place ethics at its center. To describe you in the same epideictic way, as a man of high moral principle, an ethical man in every fiber of your being. A law-abiding citizen who has been working in the same place, the G4S Security Company, for the past twenty years. A man who has received the outstanding employee award from the Ministry of Finance. I had to describe you as an empathetic man, always keen to help the poor and the needy, as a person of grace and great kindness, who, even if you did violate the law, did so inadvertently, and that that violation should be erased through that grace. As Lucius Annaeus Seneca wrote in his *Moral Epistles and Letters*, '...*everything, even if it has no beautiful element, becomes beautiful under the auspices of grace...*'"

Judge Deborah Lichtenstein acquitted me on all three charges. These are the final lines of the verdict:

"*... therefore the court rules as follows, Leonid Pekarovksy, sixty-eight years of age, a security guard, a Jew, is acquitted of all charges. All legal fees are to be met by the Israel Police.*"

The Israel Police (in other words, the State of Israel) had to pay a total of 1,500 shekels. But what was such a measly amount to the police? No more than ten agorot to a junkie. On the other hand, dear attorney Shmulik K did not charge me anything... not even a single ten agorot coin!

See You in Eden

If you asked, say, a hundred people what the oldest profession in the world is, the chances are every one of them would answer "prostitution." However, they would be wrong, having settled for an effortless, automatic reply that required the least mental strain. A more sophisticated mind, though, would ask a different question: *"Did the first man have a profession?"* And if he did, wouldn't *that* be the oldest profession in the world?

The short answer has to be yes! And not just a single profession, but two. Let's open the Bible together. The book of Genesis, Chapter 2 verse 15 says: *"Then the Lord God took the man and put him in the garden of Eden to tend and keep it…"*

There you have them both, the first and second professions. "To tend" means to be a gardener, and "to keep it" means to become a guardian of something. True, like everything else in the Book of books, those professions have purely symbolic aspects. Because what was there, really, to tend in the Garden of Eden, a garden in which all plants had been created perfect to begin with, and where there was nothing to harm them? And from whom did the first and, at that time the only, man need to keep the garden safe?

With the creation of the woman—Eve—formed from Adam's rib, the conditions for prostitution were also created. Thus it became the world's *third* oldest profession. Over time, and probably because of exceedingly high demand, it usurped the first two to claim first place, overshadowing both gardening and guarding, pushing them out. None of this means, though, that we should succumb to human feebleness, distort historical truths, and view this "first place" status as anything other than primitive self-suppression.

1

Often, my tired imagination tries to capture an image that ignites for a single moment—only to be immediately extinguished. It is the image of a not-too-young woman with traces of impressive bygone beauty. Her classic features are marked by a noble forehead, a perfectly straight nose in the classical Grecian style that contrasts with the soft curve of her lips and the firm but feminine shape of the small chin. Only her sad eyes, the color of a faded blue sky on a July day, hint at her distinguished age, and something about her suggests a magnificent aroma of wisdom.

She appears in a highly stylized British suit, a broad-brimmed, light-blue hat in the vein of Queen Elizabeth II on her head. In her hands is a small lacquered purse in a matching color.

She is my own, private *Fortuna*. Throughout the many years of my life, I still haven't been able to talk to her. I have always wanted to tell her... wanted to ask her about... never mind. No, I will still say it—I wanted to ask her about the path I do not understand. And about the goal, which is probably somewhere outside that path. And it had started so well! *Fortuna* had bestowed on me an exceptional mental airiness and a metaphysical ability to hover above it all. It was a priceless gift. Oh, the worlds I've been to! The infinite heights I have soared to!

But then, suddenly, I plunged down, like a rock. It seemed to me I was falling straight to hell but, instead, came to stand amid the gravestones of soldiers, the green surrounding them as lush as heaven's. It was the military cemetery in Holon, and I found myself in Israel—back in my ancestral homeland! A pair of garden shears appeared in my hands. I used them to trim the evergreen bushes and the low olive trees.

Well, gardener. That was my first profession in the Holy Land, just like the first man in Eden.

My boss was a Yemenite Jew called Aaron, whose name pleased my ear with its biblical intonation. He himself was something of an archeological relic. He was short in stature and, with his wide shoulders and lanky build, he echoed something ancient that had just had the layers of dust from thousands of years wiped away. His chocolaty face, with its chiseled nose, expressed kindness, and his eyes, with their pinkish whiteness, were both cunning and caressing. The hands, slightly overlong in relation to his short stature, always seemed out of step as he walked with his feet wobbling from side to side. At first glance, his hands seemed ugly, the balls of the thumbs too wide, the fingers too short and crooked. But actually, his hands were a biomechanical wonder. With the utmost skill, with superb artistic litheness, they were able to perform any task, from the simplest—planting, for example—to what, at that time, seemed to me like the most difficult task of all—fixing a lawnmower.

Aaron taught me the craft of gardening—and learning it demanded much effort and sweat. For example, weeding the wild grass, which stubbornly sprouted around the huge white and red rosebushes. The hoe had to be held in a very specific way, so that the body was bent at an angle of forty-five degrees to the earth. Even then, the stroke had to be delivered so precisely that the hoe would not dig into the ground, nor slip on it, instead severing the weed like a sharp knife. At nights, my back ached, and I rolled and twisted and turned in desperate attempts to find a comfortable position that would ease the pain. After a few months, habit took its course, and the pain began to release me from its nocturnal grip, albeit reluctantly...

The hardest task for me involved trimming the bushes. They fenced the plots of the graves in rectangular shapes, and were arranged in straight lines. The bushes constantly grew to the point of wildness, and required regular trimming. Unfortunately, I trimmed them in badly judged, crooked lines that somewhat echoed Lobachevskian geometry, in which parallel lines can meet. I think Aaron had never heard of the Russian mathematician, which was probably why he told me, rather peremptorily, that all parallel lines should actually be parallel to each other and never meet, just as the fourth axiom in Euclidian geometry demands. Utilizing several virtuosic moves I developed over time and painstakingly gained experience, I eventually achieved such perfect trimming proportions, that even Aaron was surprised.

I was in the Garden of Eden called "cemetery." I trimmed trees and bushes. I mowed the grass. I planted flowers and watered them. I swept the paths between the graves. The graves were silent. And I, who had, in the past, had a mystical horror of anything related to cemeteries, particularly to graves in which bones rested and worms squirmed, or so I imagined with great distaste, I had become used to the simple, similar stone constructs—the gravestones of soldiers.

And then one morning Aaron bid me a good morning, and asked, "Have you heard the news?"

"No. What's happened?"

"One of our northern border patrol jeeps has been blown up by a Hezbollah land mine. Two privates and a sergeant were killed. The sergeant is from Holon. The funeral is at four today. Pick up a shovel and go dig a grave!"

Aaron gave me the exact location of both plot and line. The list of tasks I was responsible for now apparently also included the digging of graves. What if I encountered a skeleton or a skull...!

I picked up a shovel and went in search of the plot and the line. On the way, I remembered a famous monologue from *Hamlet*, which I knew by heart.

"First Gravedigger: A detestable, crazy fellow, he was. Whose skull do you think it was?
Hamlet: I don't know.
First Gravedigger: A plague on him, the mad rogue! Once, he poured a pitcher of wine on my head. This skull, sir, this very skull was Yorick's, the King's jester.
Hamlet: This?
First Gravedigger: That very one.

Hamlet: Let me see it. Oh, poor Yorick! I knew him, Horatio. He had a million jokes and an excellent imagination. He let me ride on his back a thousand times. It's horrible to imagine what his back looks like now; it makes me gag. Here's where his lips hung that kissed me countless times. Where are your taunts, your games, your songs, that sense of humor that used to make the table roar with laughter? There's no one now to mock that grinning face."

I found the exact location on the right-hand upper corner of the fourth plot. I started digging and found it was easy because the graves had been pre-prepared in a particular fashion. Each plot was divided into forty graves—four rows of ten. Then they were fenced in with a low brick wall five centimeters high. A bulldozer would come onto the plot and dig, with its hydraulic blade, graves of the necessary depth and width. The walls and bottom of the grave were then coated in cement. Finally, sand would be poured in. That was it! The state in which they waited for their future, unknowing occupants.

All I had to do was dig the sand out from the grave. After about forty minutes or so, my shovel struck the cement bottom. There was no reason for any concern—I hadn't encountered any skeletons or Shakespearean skulls. A grave, shaped in the style of Futurism gaped open, ready for its new resident. I placed two planks along its length. A small mound of yellow sand waited beside it.

At four o'clock, the coffin containing the body was brought to the graveside. A large crowd gathered. At the entrance to the cemetery, people stood in a long line, preparing for the funeral procession. The chief military rabbi led the way. Behind him was an officer carrying a picture of the deceased. Four soldiers bore the coffin, which was covered by the national flag. Following them were relatives and friends… And grief, grief, grief! The kind of heart-rending grief you feel physically. And it was so pervasive it seemed to blanket the whole cemetery with a black shroud. It hung from the tree branches, it obscured the sun, it seemed to bury the whole cemetery in pitch darkness. The rabbi recited a prayer with his customary musical intonation. The beautiful mother, who led the mourners behind the coffin, shouted her grief in a heart-wrenching voice. The departed's fiancée embraced her, and also wept. There were many wreaths and flowers...

The coffin was placed on the planks over the grave. The deceased was eulogized. I can't remember what was said. I was devastated. Low in spirit. Unable to gather my conscious mind, which seemed to have been scattered in little fragments. My eyes were wet with tears, my eyesight dimmed.

Two rein-like thick ropes were slung under the coffin. It was raised as the planks were removed. Slowly, the coffin was lowered into the grave. A three-volley salute rang out, shattering the reverential silence. The mother wept in a daze.

2

When I had worked at the cemetery, I had no idea about *Fortuna's* antics. It seemed natural enough to me that a fairly young immigrant, equipped with nothing but perhaps his intellect, did a little scutwork. *I will learn the language,* I thought, *finish my new immigrant's course, find a decent job—and everything will work itself out.*

But *Fortuna*, who had pushed gardening shears into my hands and seated me on a broom like a witch, finally sent me to a guard booth.

... Oh, guarding! Will a poet ever be found, with a temperament to match Byron's, who could sing your praises? Or a historian who would depict, with a golden quill, the equal of Flavius Josephus, Livy, or Plutarch describing the atmosphere presiding within your insides—the catacombs in which the immigrant's spirit dwells...

And so, I found myself in a guard booth. A space of one meter by two. The location—southern Tel Aviv. A concrete-paved parking lot (which meant that when the temperature was thirty-five degrees Celsius everywhere else in our hot, humid country, inside the booth it would be forty). In accordance with my mood, the booth sometimes seemed to me to resemble Diogenes' barrel. Other times it would be more like an historian hermit's cell. Most often, though, it was a dungeon in which I, an innocent, had been condemned to serve a life sentence at the evil whim of some unknown person. Then I would rebel against *Fortuna,* who I was convinced had betrayed and abandoned me. My mind had been made too feeble to grasp her delicately complicated chess moves.

Well, my days in the guard's booth literally and physically crushed me. To save myself, I had to muster what little remained of my fading will, and… escape from reality. I managed to do just that. I shut down inside myself, conforming to Marcus Aurelius' doctrine, *"Dig inside yourself. Inside there is a spring of goodness ready to gush at any moment if you keep digging."* I dug vigorously. Good thing I had accumulated experience at the graveyard. Finally, I reached, with this particular shovel the other side of the wall that separated the external and internal worlds. Infinite expanses opened before my eyes, astonishing in their legendary, spectacular beauty…

I would report to the guard's booth at five in the morning— long before the scorching heat of the day set in. At that time, the night sky still hung over the city of Tel Aviv, utterly black, literally abysmal. In still life painting, I had encountered such an utter lack of color only once, at the Van Gogh Museum in Amsterdam, in the artist's last painting. Back then, I had been unable to fathom how the artist had achieved the color. Had it been through volume, created with expressive brushstrokes of thick color? Or perhaps through a barely visible contrast between the deep, pure blue Van Gogh would insert into his art in meager portions—a contrast that seemed to breathe life into the black, turning it into a living, breathing, animated organism.

I would settle in my guard's chair in the most comfortable way possible, lay my head against the headrest and close my eyes. Lines of pale light would immediately be cast on my right cheek, meticulously fashioned by the streetlight shining through the shutters.

"One doesn't have to be an artist,
But understand, it truly cuts,
As a streak of thin, small light
Pinches in the door that shuts..."

Voznesensky... What? What's this? An abyss...? Pandemonium...
Oh... I'd fallen asleep... and I mustn't sleep! There is a method for
not falling asleep. To think. Or, even better—to reflect. I slid into the
tunnel dug with my own hands...

In the twentieth century, a discussion began about stream of
consciousness and the wavelike spreading of thought. I do not experience it in quite that way. To me, it seems that thoughts leap from
particle to particle, from object to object, progressing in bounds,
in tiny portions, in quanta. There, just as you have reflected on this
thought, immediately the huge bush leaps into your mind, the one
growing by the fence on the other side of the road. The people passing it gaze straight at it but fail to see it. I asked how could anyone fail
to see it, especially in springtime, when it wears such a breathtaking
coat of white blossom, making tears spring to your eyes in some
inexplicable way. But people can't even see the sky. It is as if they are
neckless, their heads connected straight to their bodies, rendering
them unable to raise their heads.

Francis Bacon was right to say that life is mostly expressed
through the little details—but perceiving those little details, and
especially being aware of them, is very difficult. You need a keen,
sharp perception, unobscured by the vaporous film through which
only the much larger details are perceived. It "revives" the miniature
world, all those grains, all those crumbs, the petals bearing a single
drop of dew, the plaster peeling from the wall of a building, begging to tell you its story, the near-invisible flutter of the dragonfly
in the heart of south Tel Aviv's somber filth... This sharp, keen perception requires imagination; otherwise nothing marginal would
ever be interesting and possess an aesthetic value. A very small
detail, when captured by the imagination, undergoes a series of

transformations so that slowly, gradually, higher and higher levels of its beauty are revealed, until, finally, it begins to glow with luminous light, illuminated by the artist's genius. The branch of a cherry tree drawn in a scroll, for example, or a three-line *haiku*, or Kawabata's *Palm-of-the-Hand*.

So why had Blaise Pascal denied imagination so emphatically? (Here, my thoughts made yet another leap. I was sitting in the same position, the strips of light across my right cheek, my eyes closed, but sleep had been pursued by a new intellectual wind. I was afraid to startle the thought, lest the fascinating journey in the depths of my soul ceased.)

In paragraph forty-four of *The Pensées,* Pascal claims that imagination harms the intellect, and, in most instances, also reduces it. Indeed, the philosopher's claim is true for daily lives which he did not hold in a particularly high regard. Everything we are going through isn't as scary as it seems, as it appears in our imagination. The Stoics spoke about this too. Even as trouble appears in our imagination— we have already started to fear it. But perhaps it will simply pass us by, or even evaporate as it is on its way to us. In that case, the work of the imagination merely makes our lives more difficult, because of the false fear it creates.

On the other hand—and this is something Pascal doesn't discuss—there is no creation without imagination, and, as a direct result, the wholesome existence of the spirit and the sentient part of the soul are denied. Besides, is it even possible to separate— and thus discriminate—between imagination and intellect when imagination is *created* by the intellect? Through the power of the intellect, (Pascal actually writes about the opposite—about the weakness of the intellect in the face of imagination) to rein in the imagination, when it acts against it, and enhance it when it is fruitful and creative...

"Guard!!!" A thunderous voice devilishly ripped away the illusion of the morning silence. It was my boss—as coarse as life itself. How could he have known where I had just been?

"Why are you sitting in the booth?! You should be outside, welcoming the employees and customers! What do you think this is, a hotel?"

He chewed on the tips of my nerves and drank of my blood. My heart tumbled, my soul trembled. I drew a glass of water, and realized my hands were shaking, and it was only half an hour later that I finally started to calm down. However, my early morning journey had not been in vain. Actually, each similar journey, when I leave my prison booth, leaves traces on my soul. Thus, the vision becomes magnificently acute, and the thinking—which had, earlier, simply slid off the surfaces of life with indifference—now receives, surprisingly enough, an analytic grasp rife with interest. Nothing passes by my guard's booth without me dedicating some thought to it.

Firstly, human beings—who, during my fifteen years of sitting here, have passed by me in their thousands. Let us take the average Israeli, for example. What is his character? Based on what I have perceived, he is innocent, naïve and gullible. He views reality in its entirety and with complete clarity. Like a child. Or a tribesman.

He notices a detail only when it damages one of his basic character traits—his pride.

You tell me, would an average Israeli have taken any interest in the Hebrew language if it wasn't for a new immigrant, not very young, with a tiny professor's mustache, being tortured right next to him as he helplessly tried to construct a sentence? He would not miss the opportunity of saying, *"Hebrew difficult language is!"* And when the answer would come back, *"Very difficult!"* he would smile triumphantly. His pride, bloated to a gargantuan size, would have been suitably stroked.

Understanding the psychological nuances that gave birth to this pride is fairly simple. After all, it is obvious. He is in possession of something that is extremely difficult to obtain, and is, thus, priceless. Even though it is something the average Israeli has, in fact, received for free.

Hebrew does not interest him at all. He is accustomed to using it in his speech the same way he uses his teeth for chewing. He does not think about the language as a singular phenomenon; does not reflect on its antiquity, its lethargic hibernation which has lasted thousands of years. Its renewed revival and lightning-quick development. Its astonishing energy. And, at the same time its meditative, soft, romantic qualities. Its wisdom, which leans on virtuosic construction and refinement of concepts. Its elegance, its sophisticated play of light and colors in the refined works of poetry, which, with true artists, rises to the spectacular heights of the classic. The unique flair, based on the airy smells of the Mediterranean mixed with the smells of the desert, near impossible to recognize and analyze. Its intonation, which is close to that of European languages—if you make softer use of its throatier vowels…

I will admit to having said in the past, "Hebrew difficult language is!" myself. But that had been when I was waging uncompromising warfare with the language. When, in the *ulpan,* I would sink my teeth into Hebrew and it, in response, would devour its incompetent student.

Now I can say with full confidence that Hebrew, just like any other work of genius, is perfectly simple. It is, after all, perhaps the only language that has been built on the basis of pure mathematical logic, based on the principle of the golden ratio, as elegantly beautiful as ancient Greece's Parthenon. And who among us can fail to be in thrall of the aesthetic, magical play inherent in the roots of Hebrew verbs, the musical combinations of which chime like Mozart's finest improvisations…

Now that I have some familiarity with Hebrew, it mainly completes its contours in my imagination. I continue to say, by force of habit, so as not to offend anyone, "Hebrew difficult language is!" But as for the swelling of the average Israeli's pride—I rip it out by the root by asking questions like, for example, "Do you know how many words there are in the Hebrew language?"

Then I watch, almost as if I am in a theater, a mute scene. An Israeli starting to think. I try to guess at the processes of his thoughts. "Five hundred," he estimates. Because, presumably, he himself uses no more than that number. He has no need of more. But then he would remember a recent trip abroad, the many names of products in the airport duty-free stores both in Israel and in Europe, and revise his first estimate. "One thousand perhaps. Two thousand, maybe?" he hesitates. But then he recalls receiving a gift from his bank, a dictionary that contains as many as four thousand words.

"Four thousand," he says.

"No!" I say.

"What? Twenty thousand?" He is startled now.

Suddenly he begins to clearly understand that he, just like the poor new immigrant before him, has not fully mastered what he had considered to be his by right of law. This new number, twenty thousand words, has robbed him of his property.

So, I decide to show this innocent, naïve, gullible person no more mercy. "Add more! The *'Even-Shoshan Dictionary'* lists one hundred and twenty thousand words but, in fact, there are many, many more—a million and two hundred thousand!"

That's it. I see a lifeless corpse before me. My Israeli is devastated now. One million, two hundred thousand—that is a mega figure from a completely different sphere. Something indescribable, and infinite, like God himself.

Suddenly, the Israeli shows signs of life, as he endeavors to grasp at a straw. "How do you know that?"

"From the Academy of the Hebrew Language's statistical report."

That always settles the matter. The authority wielded by that particular establishment is indisputable. A journalist with sharp teeth may always try to take a bite out of the president's authority, or the Supreme Court's, but even he wouldn't dare argue with the Academy of the Hebrew Language, all too aware that its fortified castles would break his teeth...

But the deadliest question is the one that involves the most beloved word in the Hebrew language.

Even Israelis don't properly understand what this is about. For them, it is like speaking of a favorite sigh out of hundreds of thousands of identical sighs.

For me, though, as I take the philosophy of the Hebrew language very seriously, there is such a word. When I discovered it, I embraced it with the same passion felt by the Spanish conquistadors who had coveted the gold of the Incas. At first, I was surprised by its usefulness. It helped me to no end, and it made my far from simple job in the parking lot much easier. Gradually, as I used this word, I began to perceive what a treasure I now had in my possession. The word truly had magical powers. People obeyed it with their eyes closed. I think there is only one other word in the Hebrew language that is capable of having a similar effect—and that word is "Charge!" And even then, only when it is being ceaselessly shouted during some military activity to electrify warriors with intensity and strength, with energy and motivation in anticipation of the coveted victory charge. And also to demoralize the enemy troops, who, when they hear the cry, retreat so fast their pants fall to the ground.

But my magical word is "tight."

I can almost taste the disappointment you are experiencing because it is so simple a word. All I can do is ask that you refrain from judging too hastily. I'll explain everything in a second.

In the parking lot where I work as a guard, there are a limited number of parking spots. When the cars start arriving one after the other, my main task involves positioning them in the best possible way. There are three walls beside which a maximum number of cars must be parked. It is best if they are parked very close to the wall so as not to impede other cars going in and out of the lot.

I tell the drivers, "Park close to the wall." But an Israeli is no Japanese, and matters of accuracy do not interest him very much. The word "close" can be interpreted with a wide range of possibilities. It could be forty centimeters, as dictated by the laws of traffic, it could be a whole meter, or it might very well be a meter and twenty centimeters. If the distance between the car and the wall is a meter or a meter twenty when it is parked, I ask the driver to move it, in other words, park it closer to the wall. Invariably the drivers argue, as if moving their car is going to be a particularly arduous task. Some of them even shout, arguing their case at the top of their ear-splitting Mediterranean voices. Then they go and complain to the manager, and he threatens to fire me every time because, so he says, I do not know how to work with people.

But then one day... I remember it as if it was yesterday. It was a day late in the stunningly beautiful Israeli fall, very early in the morning. Dawn was painting the Tel Aviv sky a delicate crystalline light-blue, and the first sunbeams were slowly banishing the gloom of the night.

A red car stopped by the gate. I lifted the arm and said to the driver, "Park close to the wall, please." He understood, and parked the car about a meter from the wall. Then he got out of the car. He was an elderly man with gray hair, a Musketeer mustache, and a goatee. Average height, bent back. I distinctly recall how subtle the curve of his bent back was, leaving no room to doubt the nobility of its origins. It was a curve that had been formed in the quiet air of a study, accumulating millimeter by millimeter over years of intellectual occupation as its owner pored over a book or a manuscript. *Perhaps a Professor from the Tel Aviv University?* I pondered. I continued to try and assess him. A cultured person, perhaps even a left-wing intellectual. I reckoned he would start waving his arms about and shout that he had come here to buy a car, not to suffer nonsense from the guard at the gate.

He did speak, but it was in a quiet voice, in Hebrew so beautiful it was impossible not to listen to him.

When I asked him to park the car closer to the wall, he nodded and said simply, "Tight against the wall? No problem!"

Like an echo from the mountains, I repeated after him: "Tight! Tight!" and to myself I thought, *What word is this?* But then I immediately realized what it was. Between the tiles of the wall and the wheel arches of the car the elderly man left exactly three centimeters. (I wasn't lazy and actually measured the distance out of curiosity.)

And that was how I embraced the word "tight" in my personal Hebrew lexicon. With it, I became the true ruler of the parking lot. I used it like an actor practicing the Stanislavsky system.

And when I found a rhyme for it (there are poles situated opposite one of the walls of the parking lot, and the mantra I created was, *"Tight to the pole"*), the word began to glow with its own poetic colors...

I now follow a strict process. A car approaches the gate. The windows are up, of course, because the air conditioning is on. The driver can't hear me. I raise the arm of the gate, fill my lungs with air, and position the word "tight" in my throat, ready to be fired like a rocket on a launch pad.

Then, with all my might, in the lowest possible baritone voice, I thunder, "Tight to the wall!" And if there is no room by the wall, "Tight to the pole!"

This system I have developed expels the words from my throat at maximum speed—far beyond the speed of sound—and they thus possess incredible powers of penetration. My voice reaches the closed windows of the car, penetrates instantly and then impacts on the driver's head and explodes inside his brain. I see all this from his reaction. Invariably, a shiver ripples through his body, and his head jerks twice. From that moment on, his consciousness has cleared the stage for his subconscious, and he performs everything automatically, every synapse and sinew straining to accord with the word "tight," which had exploded in his head and is still reverberating there. He steers the car in a sharp maneuver toward the wall. The wheels bump into the wall tiles, one, two! He reverses and then moves the car forward again. The tires screech, the brakes groan. And, finally, the car comes to a halt, tight against the wall.

Perhaps the Hebrew language vocabulary has higher, more spiritual, or more useful words. But for me, there is no better word than "tight."

A gardener and a guard! Here's my very own *Fortuna's* plan to lead me through the course of my life on the path designed for man by God, a path not taken by the man because he had disobeyed Him. But I am marching in the opposite direction. The first man was immortal while I am mortal. He was banished from Eden because he preferred the forbidden fruit from the tree of knowledge over manual labor. In contrast, I work with the sweat of my brow, and take a taste of that same tree of knowledge only during my brief respites. As I was sitting in the guard booth, I discovered that a precious ability lies within me, the ability to put my thoughts in writing, thoughts that may be of some interest to a small part of the wider public. But that is not the main thing. The main thing is the objective! The first man and I march along different paths. He had marched away from the Garden of Eden to die upon the earth, while I tread the earth's surface—to where? *Fortuna*, am I on my way to the garden of Eden?

Well, in that case, I'll see you in Eden.

Transplant

"Are you Jewish?"

"You bet!"

"You must be circumcised."

"Yes and no."

"How come?"

"It goes like this: first, they circumcised me... then I restored it."

"Wait, wait! This is interesting. Give me the details."

"When we arrived in Israel, there was a lot of talk about 'circumcised' or 'uncircumcised,' 'brith or no brith.' The Bukharans and others who came from small towns walked proudly with their heads held high; one hundred percent *kosher*. While we, who came from the big cities—Moscow, Leningrad, Kiev—walked around with our heads bent low.

"The rabbi tried to convince us. 'This is the Lord's will. The terms that made the Jews the chosen people.'

"On the other hand, the leftist intellectuals said, 'Your rabbi is talking nonsense. This whole circumcision thing is just about hygiene. Just imagine, the ancient near East, desert, unbearable heat, sweat. Dirt accumulates. Infection. That is where it all started...'

"Forgive me, distinguished leftist intellectuals, what are you actually saying here? In the ancient near East, ears never got dirty? They did? Well, then, let's cut them too while we're at it! What about the nails? Let's tear them out! Did you forget about sweaty feet? We need to shower much more. Two or three times a day, at least...

"Nothing could convince me. Besides, I was a little worried—after all, an operation was involved. And I had no real need of it. In the end, it took my wife to convince me.

87

"'Understand,' she said, 'the rabbi is right. Why, can you not imagine that this way, being circumcised, you will be closer to God? And the leftist intellectuals are right as well, dirt does accumulate under the foreskin. But that isn't the main thing. What's important is that a *brith* will bring something new with it—an overwhelming urge that will breathe new life into our worn-out love life. It will be so cute, your naked smooshy!'

"Then came the hospital. Local anesthesia. Three days of unpaid vacation. Ten days of crawling like a lobster with open claws, wife waiting patiently till it all healed.

"'Well, what do you think?'

"'It's a little inexpressive.'

"As for what happened after that... God, it scares me to even think about it! Tears, bouts of hysteria and depression; oh yes, the depression! Nothing was right for her. I was both wilted and dried up. I had nothing of the passion I used to have. Even my touch now felt artificial and anemic to her. And—what was most infuriating—she couldn't *feel* me. No more talk about 'new urges' and my 'naked smooshy.' We had to salvage things. The family could have fallen apart. And that really was the situation. The wife was angry like some ravenous she-wolf, and I—like a beaten dog— was apparently to blame for everything. Access to her body was, of course, denied...

"And then, suddenly, unexpectedly, the solution appeared— once again, thanks to my wife's resourcefulness.

"'Do you remember Irka Shamonina?' she asked one day, as if coincidentally. 'The woman who surgically restored her virginity just before her wedding with Givoy? Why don't you restore yours as well?'

"'What do you mean 'restore'? Irka Shamonina is one thing, while I'm a different story altogether. You think they have such surgeries for circumcised men now?'

"'Oh, come on! If they can transplant hearts, kidneys and livers, surely they can restore your miserable foreskin?'

"'Miserable!' Outwardly, I pretended to be insulted, but it wasn't long before I went to the Beilinson Hospital in Petah Tikva, known to be the finest skin-grafting establishment in the country, to restore my foreskin—and get some domestic peace.

"In the hospital, the entire plastic surgery department flocked to see me.

"'What, are you insane?' they asked. 'Here, in the only Jewish state in the world, you want to stitch your foreskin up instead of cutting it? You really are out of your mind, and... and...' (they paused, searching for the right word) 'you're... you're a villain!'

"I got the same reaction in all the other hospitals. In Jerusalem, Tel Aviv, Beersheba. It became obvious to me that restoring my foreskin—at least in Israel—was going to be impossible.

"'Fly to the Netherlands,' my wife said coolly. 'I already checked. In Amsterdam, there's a clinic where they do sex-change operations. For them, solving our little problem would be nothing.'

"'And the money?'

"'We'll take out a loan.'

"So we took out a loan, and I flew to Amsterdam. Not far from Square Dam, one of the most beautiful in Europe, I found the sex-change clinic. It was actually based in a magnificent seventeenth-century palace beside a picturesque canal. In a lobby rich with greenery reflected in mirrors, there roamed, so I imagined, transgenders with made-up eyes and plucked eyebrows, and others with little mustaches and tiny sideburns.

"I was admitted by none other than Professor Van der Stool himself.

"'How can I help you?' the professor asked.

"I explained. He looked at me, considering.

"'So, are you doing a lot of these surgeries?' I was starting to feel a little stressed, fearing another of the many refusals I'd encountered in Israel.

"'I must admit,' the professor said, 'this is the first such request I've come across. However, technically, there shouldn't be a problem.

The only possible hitch I can foresee is finding a donor. Once things become clearer, we'll call you.'

"I sat in my hotel room and waited for a phone call. A day passed. Then two, and then three—and still nothing. I was beginning to feel worried. Then, just before the weekend, the phone finally rang. Van der Stool.

"'Just as I thought, finding a donor proved to be a difficult matter. Hardly anyone was willing to do a *brith*. But we managed to convince a man from the Central African Republic. If you are happy with that, be here tomorrow at 10:00 a.m.'

"I called my wife. There was a thirty-second pause as she weighed all the considerations for and against.

"'Say yes! We don't really have a choice—not after all the money we've spent.'

"I must here put in a good word or two about Professor Van der Stool's skill. Good hands. One of the greatest experts in Europe. My wife is convinced he is actually a great artist. As a former art researcher, she easily finds juicy descriptions for his work of art. It is both a *'bio-energetic wonder,'* and an *'object with a subtle combination of colors.' 'The contrast between the dark chocolate color and the shades of the bright fragrant, imbues the entire spectrum with a unique erotic touch. It is also a new movement in kinetic art, a movement that influences the form—and a Hellenistic-style sculpture with a perfect balance between weight and volume.'*

"All wonderful words she showered on Professor Van der Stool's work. It is as if I had nothing at all to do with it, though I have to say there is something in it for me after all, as there are moments when she calls me, in times of excitement, 'You African savage!' and 'Oh, you cannibal...'"

"Truly a fascinating story. One might even call it unique. With your permission, I will write it down."

"With pleasure."

Gravestone

Yitzhak Koula, an elderly Jewish-Romanian, visits his son's grave regularly, three times a week, at the Military Cemetery in Holon. A twenty-year-old boy, an only child, Yitzhak's son had died in the *Yom Kippur* War. Since then, his parents' lives had become meaningless. Koula's appearance does not make him stand out. He is tall and skinny and he has a grayish, narrow face. His gait is awkward, and he shuffles his feet as he walks. When he relates the story of his son, Yitzhak's feeble voice trembles and sorrowful tears well in his reddening eyes, like water, like swamp water. The area around the flower-strewn grave is always perfectly clean, but Koula, with ritualistic fervor, sweeps the tiles with a hard brush anyway. Then he lights a memorial candle, places it in a lantern-like glass fixture, opens a prayerbook, closes his eyes and starts rocking back and forth as he silently says *kaddish*. After the prayer, he takes a small light-blue pail and vanishes through the gate that separates the military cemetery from the civilian.

I once asked Koula why he goes to the civilian cemetery. So one day the old man led me through the gate to show me. It turned out that not far from his son's grave, he had brought a plot for himself and his wife—which was a pretty obvious thing for him to do. What amazed me, though, was another matter entirely. When we got to the future resting place of Koula and his wife I noticed two large sarcophagi made of fine marble, carved from the mountains of Judea. They were connected by a five-foot slab of black, polished marble. On it, in bronze letters, were carved the words, "*Here Lie Yitzhak and Esther Koula.*"

I stood and thought about the old Romanian-Jew Yitzhak Koula, whose life had been turned to ashes by the Holocaust and the

91

death of his son. And I realized that even though it had become bitter ashes, life still surged in his feeble body—after all, it was still possible to touch Koula, speak to him, still look into his reddening eyes. But this lavish gravestone—a trademark of death's manifestation—severed any attempt to think about Koula as a living human being. This monument—the first of its kind in the overcrowded cemetery—is as tangible as all the other marble gravestones, and as natural as sand, as the lifeless landscape that surrounds it, like the two deceased beneath the stone.

Wait! Koula is still alive! He's right beside me. Though death has already put his name on his list, and Koula appears to be gone. But no, no! He's alive, and this attempt of his to pre-arrange his eternal home, is not as naïve as it seems...

Koula, meanwhile, is gently brushing the surface of marble and granite from whose black mirror surface glittering sparks splash into the steaming air. Sparks that fly into Koula's eyes, igniting a white fire there that no longer belongs to this world. His features change, reflecting a quiet, tender happiness. And all of this combines to demonstrate that the perpetual pain momentarily releases Koula. He lovingly waters the jasmine bushes. He returns the pail to its place. Then he leaves me and walks tall towards his car. Before he drives away, he casts another appeasing glance at his own lavish grave.

Borscht

Four prostitutes from Ukraine—Olsia, Galia, Natasha and Lena—had a craving for Ukrainian borscht. Oh, how tired they were of Arab-Israeli cuisine; all that hummus and falafel and shawarma! And bananas, which at first they had consumed by the dozen, were actually making them sick to their stomachs, like in pregnancy. And their hips had started to swell too, forming unsightly bumps commonly called "love handles."

And that Ukrainian borscht...

The rich purple color, like a forest in autumn on the outskirts of Kiev... Steaming clouds of aromatic vapor billowing up from the plate, broadcasting the scent of tomato paste, cabbage, carrot, and cooked beef that fell off the sugar-white bone merely from the sound of smacking lips. Add a spoonful of white country cream, almost as hard as butter, and a slice of fresh, black Ukrainian bread after the hard crust has been rubbed with a clove of garlic...

And, at the mere thought of the incomparable taste of Ukrainian borscht with black bread and garlic, the mouths of the four prostitutes flooded with saliva, which they gulped down with relish.

A middle-aged poetess, who reads her love poetry with whiny pathos as she rolls her eyes skyward and presses her hands to her chest, would wrinkle her nose in distaste. How rude! Why so vulgar? Prostitutes? But they, after all, are the servants of the love goddess. Her priestesses!

Unfortunately, the four Ukrainian girls looked nothing like the priestesses of love. Their faces were swollen. Their skin was white, but far from fresh. Their figures were all bent. The first possessed sagging breasts. The second had buttocks that hung too low. The third had crooked legs. And no one would have wanted to gaze into the eyes of the fourth—empty, like the holes in the eyes of the statues of ancient Rome: without soul, brain, or heart.

But we all know who the original priestesses of love were. They were called *"hetaeras"* in ancient Greece. Their proportions were perfect. Their beauty dazzling. After all, they had served as models for ancient Greek sculptors, such as Phidias, for example, or Polykleitos, whose art thrills us to this very day. They were the confidants of ancient Greek warlords and philosophers. Their intellects dazzled with sharpness and wit, and their souls—with mesmerizing sensuality. If it hadn't been like that, how else would history still remember, more than two thousand years later, their names, which we still speak of with admiration? Laontium, Phryne, Erotia and Pythionisia.

But there was another who overshadowed them all, the legendary Aspasia, the wife of Pericles, that giant of statesmanship whose name defines the classic age of Greek civilization, the golden age of Greek culture and art. She entered the annals of world history thanks to Plato and Plutarch. And thus wrote the Greek historian in the book that relates the history of Pericles' life:

"... She was born in the city of Miletus, and was the daughter of Axiochus. They say she had followed in the footsteps of an ancient Ionian woman named Traglia, and had ties only with men of the highest social orders. Pericles was charmed by her wisdom and her knowledge of political matters. Socrates, too, would sometimes come to see her with his acquaintances, and his disciples would bring their wives to her to bask in her wisdom, despite the fact that her profession was not counted among the beautiful or respectable, for she managed a group of young prostitutes..."

And now let us hear the words of Socrates, who, in one of the early Socratic dialogues written by Plato, *Menexenus*, is having a conversation about the art of oratory with a youth named Menexenus, son of Demophon:

MENEXENUS: Do you think you could speak yourself if there should be a necessity, and if the council were to choose you?

SOCRATES: That I should be able to speak is no great wonder, Menexenus, considering that I have an excellent mistress in the art of rhetoric. She who has made so many good speakers, and one who was the best among all the Hellenes—Pericles, the son of Xanthippus. MENEXENUS: And who is she? I suppose you mean Aspasia. SOCRATES: Yes, I do. And besides her I had Connus, the son of Metrobius, as a master, and he was my master in music as she was in rhetoric. MENEXENUS: Truly, Socrates, I marvel that Aspasia, who is only a woman, should be able to compose such a speech. She must be a rare one. SOCRATES: Well, if you are incredulous, you may come with me and hear her... MENEXENUS: I have often met Aspasia, Socrates, and I know what she is like...

Such were the priestesses of love, my distinguished lady poetess, while our prostitutes were simply damaged and illegal goods. And they roamed the criminal neighborhood renowned throughout the country—the Tel Aviv Old Central Bus Station—and resided in massage parlors, thus named only to disguise themselves in a sophisticated manner.

But this wasn't about massage, and certainly wasn't about a whorehouse. It was more like a crime den, that lurked on the first floor of a dilapidated, crumbling building. Instead of a door, there was a red curtain that masqueraded as brocade. Beyond the red curtain was a reception room. About twenty meters square, its walls painted a poisonous green. In the corner stood a table and a chair with crooked legs, and behind the table sat the "Madame"—a mustachioed woman called Fira. A tattered sofa, three ancient armchairs, and a low table were the only other items of furniture. A shelf was attached to the wall, a television atop it.

Most of the time, the prostitutes sat on the sofa and the armchairs, making themselves look pretty as they watched Russian shows on the television. From the reception room a door led to a shabby corridor, and from there other doors led into four narrow rooms, which were separated from each other by thin plaster walls. In each room there was a bed and a chair on which the customers draped their clothes. On the other side of the corridor there was a shower, several dismal restrooms, and a small kitchen.

In the kitchen, on a stove, rested a medium-sized pot with Ukrainian borscht cooking in it. Olsia had been entrusted with the task of overseeing the borscht. As a prostitute, she wasn't much to talk about, but as a cook she was quite talented. Olsia ran from the reception room to the kitchen to taste the borscht with a spoon. If it had been golden Jewish chicken soup, it would have been tinted red with Olsia's lipstick, which covered her lips in a thick layer. However, borscht is also crimson in color, so that Olsia dipping her lips into the pot left no marks or traces.

Eventually the vegetables and meat were cooked through, and the steaming liquid had absorbed their flavors.

"Ready!" Olsia joyously screamed from the kitchen.

Then she carried the pot to the reception room and placed it on the low table. The others moved the sofa and armchairs nearer. Even the Madame, Fira, dragged her crooked-legged chair over and, after locking the cash register, went and sat at the low table. They sat there expectantly, all in their working clothes—brassieres and knickers. Fira was the only one wearing a dress. Olsia poured the soup into the deep bowls, the rich aroma crackling into their nostrils like fireworks. They sliced the bread. They peeled the garlic. Then they ate in silence. Sanctifying the moment.

Suddenly—a slight shiver ruffled the red curtain.

Please, let it not be him, thought Olsia in shock. But it was. The curtain shifted, lifted to one side, and into the reception room— which was currently serving as the dining room—walked Rabbi Shimon Brechter. The *yeshivah* students called this wise and learned man SB, and thought his intuition and sophistication literally super-human. Olsia, though—SB being one of her regulars—had given him the more derisive nickname, which also contained no little primal fear—"The Piston," because of his inconceivable virility. *God damn him to hell,* she thought. And thanks to her profession, Olsia had enough data to make comparisons. One piston, according to her calculations, was the equivalent of three illegal workers from Romania, or four Arabs from the territories, or five Chinese. But those were her own personal, subjective notions. For our part, we will attempt to appreciate Rabbi Shimon Brechter from a different side, to gain an entirely objective view.

He was actually handsome! Radiating so much in his freshness and righteousness that one could easily have mistaken him for Santa Claus himself, that is, if SB hadn't been a representative of Orthodox Judaism's most extreme faction—the Breslov Hassids. Despite all that, the Rabbi was an aesthete. Down his shapely body flowed the quick lines of his almost perfectly sewn coat. The round hat, whose expensive fur indicated "The Piston's" lofty position, was recollective, with its regal weight, of the hat that had belonged to Monomakh, Prince of Kiev. And the white socks, exposed somewhere in the area of the knees, below the tight pants, disappeared into black Italian shoes of the highest quality, a genuine work of plastic art.

And the Rabbi's face was like a portrait sculpted by the hand of Michelangelo Buonarroti—so harmonious was his image. And the colors, the colors! The portrait must have been made of Carrara marble, with its perfect shade, and the pinkish, almost invisible adornments.

But what of the silvery beard, which ended right below the upper lip with the curling roof of a mighty Nietzschean mustache. It wasn't a complete, uniform unit like Moses's biblical beard, created under Michelangelo's skillful hand. SB's beard was meticulously cultivated and groomed, combed and parted in the middle. A real Bernard Shaw. The lines of the forehead and nose were also similar, and so were the eyes that blazed powerfully blue, and from whose depths reflected a clever shrewdness, devoid, though, of Bernard Shaw's sarcasm.

During the time he had studied in the *yeshiva*, that shrewd cleverness had nearly ruined the Rabbi's life. During his time there, SB had experienced a deep spiritual crisis. Being one of the most gifted students, he had faced a seemingly unsolvable dilemma: which way should he go? The way of entirely melting into the faith, eschewing any criticism to the verge of absurdity, or, alternatively, and in a manner more fitting to the philosophical inclination of his thinking—in a way of rationally attempting to explain the Creation, following the path traced by Rashi and Maimonides. These two alternatives negated each other, and it seemed to the Rabbi that his inability to make a decision could cause him to stray from the path of the faithful altogether.

But God, so the Rabbi thought, had indicated a third, utterly unique way for him. One that would allow him to slip between "Scylla and Charybdis," between blind faith and its rational understanding. It was not for nothing that the Almighty had gifted SB with an omnipotent virility, and a vastly superior erotic imagination; an imagination that could sweep the Rabbi through the corridor of reality straight into the higher realms. That was his vast and guarded secret. From that secret all his spiritual revelations emanated, which, in turn, quenched the thirst in his soul.

And what of the failed prostitute Olsia, whom nature had created in a moment of tiredness and apathy? Was her derelict body the corridor that connected SB with infinite spirituality? Exactly! And now there was Olsia, lying in the usual position which ignited, like a spark, The Piston's imagination. Her feminine form, too sharply defined and tangible, began to melt in SB's scorching consciousness, then melted altogether. The fire blazed hotter and hotter inside The Piston, as if some invisible hand was ceaselessly feeding coal into his steam engine. And all that pent-up energy wanted to burst out, despite the monotonous nature of the Rabbi's motions—back and forth, back and forth.

The naïve Olsia had always marveled at their primal nature. But that was precisely where the essence of SB's sophisticated skill lay.

Because the highest form of sexual simplicity was the same erotic simplicity The Piston aspired to, and which he was able to achieve. Perfection limited the subconscious aspiration for releasing methods of indulgence, and focused all of SB's will in the spiritual energy bound by the material, so he could unwind this energy and allow it to take flight and soar into the most elevated heights.

As for Olsia, other than the mighty pounding that rattled her entire body, she felt pain as well. And a "slushing" of borscht in her stomach. And a discharge of garlic that aspired to burst.

"When will this all be over?" the prostitute quietly whispered.

But it wasn't over for a very long time. The Piston entered a state of a most powerful erotic ecstasy which slowly poured out in a thick honey-colored flow, out of his back and forth movements.

But all things have their beginning and endings. SB's silvery, springy sidelocks were moving faster and faster. Then as rapidly as they possibly could, and a long wolf howl rattled the crime den.

"Ah-wooooooo…"

In the reception room, everyone was already familiar with The Piston's habits. Everyone realized he had been "unburdened." And truly, SB, as sated and full as a leech that had suckled its fair share of blood, detached from Olsia and rolled over beside her to lie on his back. He lay like that for about ten minutes, unmoving, his eyes closed. Then he jumped up as if nothing had happened, dressed, and rushed out with a spring in his step.

Olsia went to shower. The next day she would have a day off—after The Piston, she thought she deserved a vacation. She put on bra and panties and went out to the reception room. Her plate was the only one still on the low table, still filled with the borscht that had already cooled, the surface coated with a layer of fat. Olsia felt nauseous. She did not feel like eating. But no one throws borscht away, and, somehow, she managed to finish it. Then she went to the kitchen and washed the plate.

Guard Booth
A Modern, Middle Eastern
Fairytale

Once upon a time, in a faraway Middle Eastern, democratic country, there lived a guard. The guard spent whole days sitting in a booth that stood sentinel over a concrete parking lot situated in the southern part of a beautiful city beside the Mediterranean Sea. Now, the guard did not care for the booth because it reminded him of a prison dungeon. And indeed, the booth measured just one meter by two. Bars had been installed on all three windows, and the iron door provided a surface which, in the daylight hours of summer—and summer lasted nine months of the year in that southern country—invariably heated to a temperature of 35-40 degrees Celsius. Often, the guard would address a question to a certain gentleman—elegant rather than young—who was, in fact, none other than his own fate. "Why have you seen fit to place me in this booth?" The gentleman, though, always remained silent, merely smiling mysteriously.

However, the guard had not been born to sit in the booth. He was certain there were greater abilities and powers within himself. He knew that if only the democratic country knew about them, and utilized those powers and those abilities, it would have gained much. But the democratic country had no need of that—not of the guard himself, nor of his powers and abilities. Which was why, every morning, at seven o'clock exactly, he would arrive to sit, sweltering, in the booth in the concrete car park.

100

Later, his boss, the manager of the car park, would show up and say, "Guard, come here! Are you not aware of your duties? You must be in the booth, by the telephone. I've been calling and calling, and no one has picked up!"

After the manager, the clients of the company that owned the concrete parking lot would follow. And they would say, albeit with slightly less aggression than the manager, "Guard, come on! Lift the barrier arm, quick!"

And so, it went on, year after year. The guard sat in the booth like a prisoner sentenced to life because he had committed some horrible crime.

And then, one day, after he had occupied the booth for ten years and ten months, something inexplicable happened to the guard. As if his eyes had been opened, he began to observe things he hadn't seen before, sense scents he hadn't smelled before. He heard nature's music to which he had been deaf. His heart filled to the brim with love, with no room left in it for pain and despair. A whole new kaleidoscope of lofty, beautiful thoughts darted and swirled in his head.

Eventually, the guard decided to start writing his thoughts down. And though it proved very difficult, he managed to write his story. And it turned out very well, though the guard did not know it at first. He sent the story to a certain literary supplement where he knew talent was appreciated. And there, the story came to a wizard's attention. The wizard had been waiting for the story for ten years and ten months, from the day fate had placed the guard in the booth, in fact. The wizard published the story in his magical literary supplement, adding a few magical words about the guard.

Many people read the story. All were surprised that such a wonderful story had been written by a simple guard sitting in an ancient booth in a concrete car park. They started visiting the car park and the guard, to see for themselves that he truly existed, and that this was not some publicity prank being played by the distinguished wizard.

What else is there to say? Even the guard's boss stopped shouting at him in the mornings. And the more senior managers found ways to praise him. It was all a measure of how accomplished the story the guard had written was!

Word of this special guard spread far and wide until it eventually reached the ear of the big boss himself, the owner of the company. The boss happened to be a great literary connoisseur. Which was why it was quite natural for him to love the story very much and treat the guard's talent with the highest regard.

One day, the big boss invited the guard to his spacious office. He told him, "Guard, you wrote a wonderful story. It gave me much enjoyment. You may ask whatever your heart pleases from me!"

The guard, tired of sitting like a felon in an old, tiny booth, said, "I thank you for your compliments. If possible, I would like a new booth!"

"Your booth will be replaced," the big boss said.

The next day, laborers appeared at the concrete car park and dismantled the old booth that resembled a dungeon. In its place they erected a new booth, a virtual palace. The new booth was built using dark-red terracotta bricks, and topped with a roof of orange, Dutch roof tiles and rounded edges, like a Chinese pagoda. The three windows were brought to life with wooden decorations, and the façade of the otherwise plain wooden door was relieved by the addition of an attractive wooden carving. The interior design was just as opulent. The floor was marble tiles with sophisticated mosaics, a couch and sofa of Italian leather were installed, as were a small mahogany table, a small refrigerator, a computer and an air conditioner...

The guard took possession of his new booth—and from the day he first sat in it, inspiration left him. He never wrote another line.

60846084R00060